TREASURES
OF THE
AQUARIANS

TREASURES OF THE AQUARIANS

The Sixties Discovered

Richard Davis and Jeff Stone

The Complete Exhibit Catalog
of the Berkeley Dig

PENGUIN BOOKS

PENGUIN BOOKS
Viking Penguin Inc., 40 West 23rd Street,
New York, New York 10010, U.S.A.
Penguin Books Canada Limited, 2801 John Street,
Markham, Ontario, Canada L3R 1B4

First published in Penguin Books 1985

Published simultaneously in Canada

An East Chelsea Press Book
Printed in the United States of America
Design by Ken Diamond, Art Patrol/NYC
Original photographs by Leighton Miller

CONTENTS

Primary Dig Site

INTRODUCTION

A startling and important archaeological discovery was recently made in the area of our planet once known as California, when a cache of artifacts dating from the 1960s was unearthed, relatively intact, during the building of the transglobal tunnel. The best scholars from a score of disciplines—including archaeology, history, languages and anthropology—have studied and interpreted these artifacts and have mounted an exhibition that will open at the Metroplex Museum of Art in the fall. Never has so great a body of information been available about a time and culture of which we have previously known so little.

The artifacts were uncovered by a construction crew in the ruins of a postindustrial town known as Berkeley ("zip code" coordinate 94704). Experts quickly determined that what the workers had stumbled upon was not merely a small, isolated find—significant as that would have been, considering our extremely limited knowledge of the 1960s—but the largest group of mid-twentieth-century dwelling foundations ever discovered, together with their stunning contents. Miraculously, these remains were not pulverized by the ground undulations known to have shaken the Berkeley region throughout the twentieth and twenty-first centuries.

The primary dig site comprised an area approximately 105 yards long by 44 yards wide. Additional objects were discovered as much as one quarter of a mile away, in an area believed to have been the location of the University of California at Berkeley. At the height of its splendor in the 1960s, the university was perhaps the greatest seat of learning in western North Amerika. Unfortunately, practically nothing of the great institution remains, but its grandeur is legendary. The campus alone was the size of a small city, with its classrooms, laboratories, stadia and great public squares, all of which played an essential role in the dramatic events of the 1960s.

Berkeley was the crossroads of cataclysmic but only dimly understood social, political and cultural changes that rocked the civilization of the Western Hemisphere to its very foundations. Home to thousands of students, spiritual seekers, artisans, traders, functionaries, cult leaders and vagabonds known as "street people," Berkeley was the magnet city of its time. Consequently, the artifacts of the 1960s discovered there are unmatched in richness and variety and as a source for our understanding of that distant time.

Little is known of the societies that neighbored the Berkeley civilization. Evidently, a people called the Amerikans, whose values were in many ways antithetical to those of the Berkeleyites, shared the midsection of the North Amerikan continent with them. The boundaries between the two groups apparently were not clearly defined, resulting in numerous border skirmishes and several major battles.

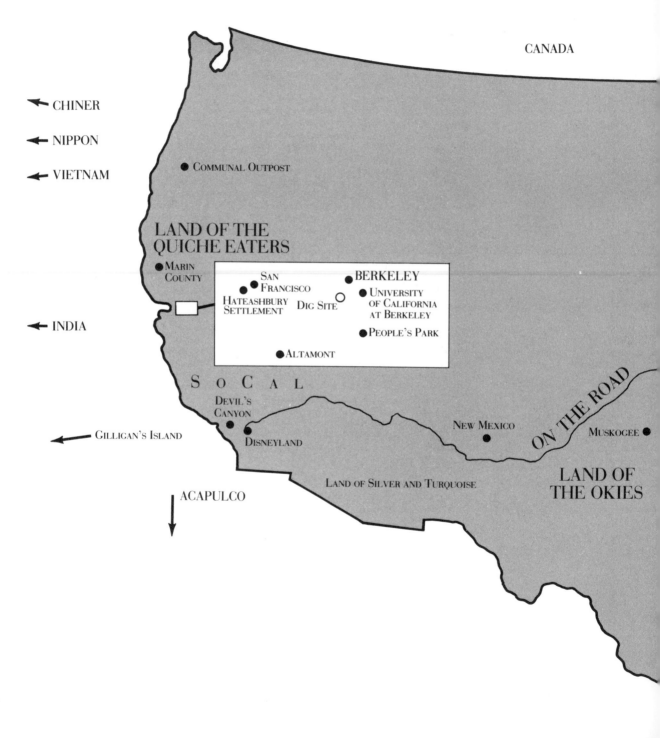

CHINER

NIPPON

VIETNAM

CANADA

● COMMUNAL OUTPOST

LAND OF THE
QUICHE EATERS

● MARIN
COUNTY

SAN
FRANCISCO

BERKELEY

HATEASHBURY
SETTLEMENT

DIG SITE

● UNIVERSITY
OF CALIFORNIA
AT BERKELEY

INDIA

● PEOPLE'S PARK

● ALTAMONT

S o C A L

DEVIL'S
CANYON

GILLIGAN'S ISLAND

DISNEYLAND

NEW MEXICO

ON THE ROAD

MUSKOGEE ●

LAND OF
THE OKIES

ACAPULCO

LAND OF SILVER AND TURQUOISE

AMERIKA IN THE AQUARIAN AGE

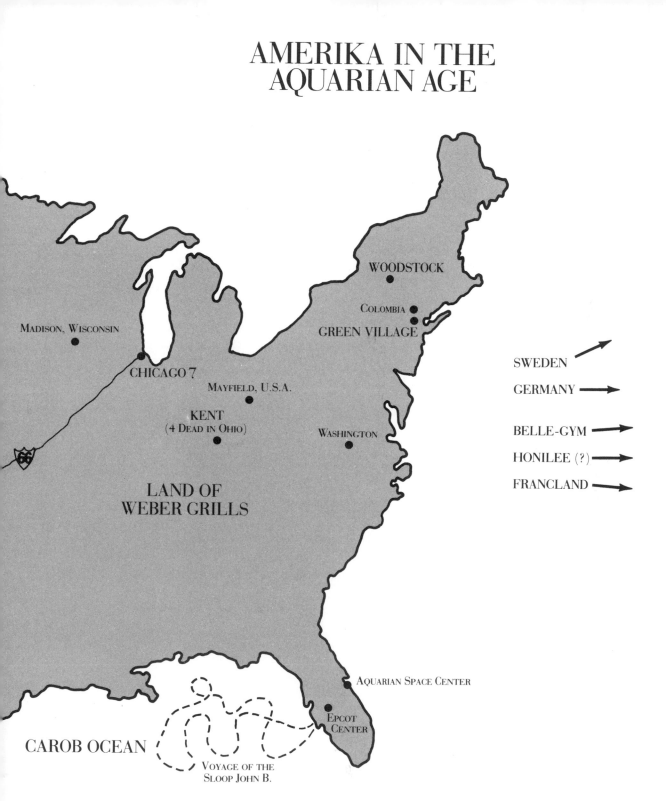

WOODSTOCK

COLOMBIA
GREEN VILLAGE

MADISON, WISCONSIN

CHICAGO 7

MAYFIELD, U.S.A.

KENT
(4 DEAD IN OHIO)

WASHINGTON

66

LAND OF
WEBER GRILLS

SWEDEN
GERMANY

BELLE-GYM

HONILEE (?)

FRANCLAND

AQUARIAN SPACE CENTER

EPCOT
CENTER

CAROB OCEAN

VOYAGE OF THE
SLOOP JOHN B.

The Berkeley artifacts were not without hazards, particularly the ones later determined to be primitive drugs and explosive weapons. Yet many of the researchers developed a genuine fondness and respect for the Berkeleyites, whom they refer to as Aquarians. The name is derived from a song recorded on a grooved plastic disk discovered at the dig site. (Several such objects were found and were eventually identified by specialists as "phonograph records.") A favorite of the dig personnel, this song heralded the beginning of the "Age of Aquarius."

I invite you to journey with us now many thousands of years back into the deep recesses of time. It is my hope that you too will come to think of the Aquarians in more familiar terms, perhaps as rather peculiar but valued friends. It is all too easy, in our age of wide-ranging space exploration and colonization, to focus too closely on their idiosyncrasies, and so lose sight of the common humanity they so clearly share with ourselves.

—THOMAS HEAVING DIGGERHALTER
Curator, North Amerikan Antiquities
Metroplex Museum of Art

TIMELINE OF THE AQUARIAN AGE

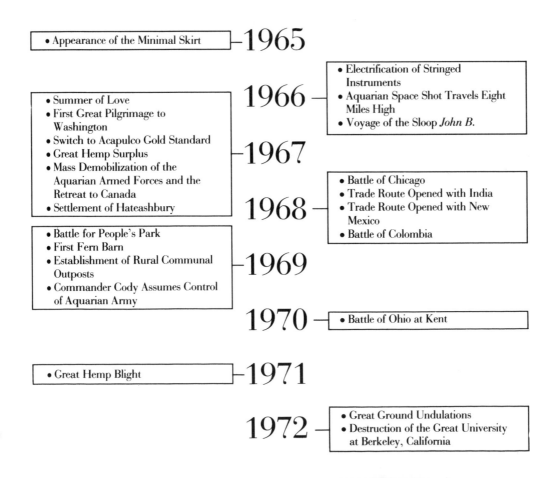

1965
• Appearance of the Minimal Skirt

1966
• Electrification of Stringed Instruments
• Aquarian Space Shot Travels Eight Miles High
• Voyage of the Sloop *John B.*

1967
• Summer of Love
• First Great Pilgrimage to Washington
• Switch to Acapulco Gold Standard
• Great Hemp Surplus
• Mass Demobilization of the Aquarian Armed Forces and the Retreat to Canada
• Settlement of Hateashbury

1968
• Battle of Chicago
• Trade Route Opened with India
• Trade Route Opened with New Mexico
• Battle of Colombia

1969
• Battle for People's Park
• First Fern Barn
• Establishment of Rural Communal Outposts
• Commander Cody Assumes Control of Aquarian Army

1970
• Battle of Ohio at Kent

1971
• Great Hemp Blight

1972
• Great Ground Undulations
• Destruction of the Great University at Berkeley, California

"When the revolution comes . . ."

"How can we lose when we're so sincere?"

—Ancient Aquarian Proverbs

CHAPTER 1

THE HOME AND DOMESTIC ARTS

ITEM P3
WHAM-O PLATE
PLASTIC
DIMENSIONS: Diameter 9″
MINT CONDITION

LIKE THE great plate makers of the eighteenth and nineteenth centuries, the Aquarians excelled in the art of creating fine dinnerware. Working in "plastic," the medium of the time, the Aquarians created a strong yet highly decorative plate.

The example pictured above was found in excellent shape, a lasting testament to the durability of Aquarian plates. Unlike plates and pottery from other ancient cultures, the Aquarian plate is not cracked or otherwise marred.

The underside of the plate is grooved, bears a laurel leaf design and the plate-maker's mark, **Wham-O.** This plate was inscribed **Regular Frisbee R,** which is assumed to be the plate-maker's code for this particular edition.

The plate also contains information on place of origin (San Gabriel, California), an identification number (3,359,678) and a motto that must have appealed to the free-spirited Aquarians: PLAY CATCH—INVENT GAMES.

Scientists have marveled at the uncanny resemblance the plate bears to the X-25 space transport.

GLASS JAR, GRAIN PRODUCT

GLASS, METAL, PAPER LABEL
DIMENSIONS: 6″ × 12″
INSCRIPTION: "Brown Rice"

THE RECOVERY of fragments from the book *Diet for a Small Planet*, which advocates the eating of grains and vegetables, offered valuable insights into Aquarian food consumption patterns.

The dig site offered several large glass jars containing vegetable and grain products. No animal bones, Weber grills or other evidence of flesh consumption were discovered.

The only known exception to the Aquarians' vegetarian eating habits is indicated by the discovery of a menu from The Pall Mall Cocktail Lounge, San Francisco. The menu included an item known as a "Love Burger—a quarter pound of 100 percent ground beef on your choice of white or whole wheat bun. Groove on it."

14

ARM & HAMMER®
BAKING SODA

PAPER, INK, BICARBONATE OF SODA	
DIMENSIONS: 4″ × 5″ × 1¹/₂″	
NET WEIGHT: 16 ounces (1 pound)	
INSCRIPTION: "A pure and natural product for over 125 years"	

THIS HUMBLE product was one of the most common of Aquarian household goods. The example pictured here was found on a wire rack inside a large metal cabinet attached to a cooling device evidently designed to keep the baking soda at the optimum temperature.

The Aquarians valued **Arm & Hammer®** Baking Soda for its simple, wholesome character, and especially for its versatility. It could be used for brushing the teeth, for household cleaning, as foot powder, even in cooking.

The origin of the symbol imprinted on the cheerful red-and-yellow box is not known for certain, but some suspect that it may be found in a song recorded by the troubadors **Pete, Paul and Marie,** "If I Had a Hammer." The song mentions hammering in the "morning," "evening," and "all over this land," hinting at the many uses to which Arm & Hammer® Baking Soda might be put.

15

MACRAMÉ WAS apparently one of the most flourishing of the abundant Aquarian handicraft industries. Found at the dig site were articles of nearly every size, shape and possible purpose—aesthetic as well as utilitarian—created by this process.

The most common of all the macramé objects discovered were hanging holders. Specialists are not quite certain what they were intended to hold—perhaps stacked Wham-O plates or other kitchen vessels. The knots and beads that decorated the holders may have enabled them to serve as primitive counting devices as well, perhaps keeping track of food supply levels. In any case, the Aquarians must have been adept at ducking, dodging movements, for the holders undoubtedly created something of a hanging obstacle course.

Macramé products were made largely from vegetable fibers indigenous to the Berkeley area, especially the highly venerated hemp plant. Anthropologists believe the Aquarians may have combined ritual-drug ceremonies with spring festivals of renewal by burning old macramé objects and inhaling the smoke.

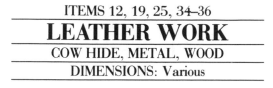

LEATHER WORK

COW HIDE, METAL, WOOD

DIMENSIONS: Various

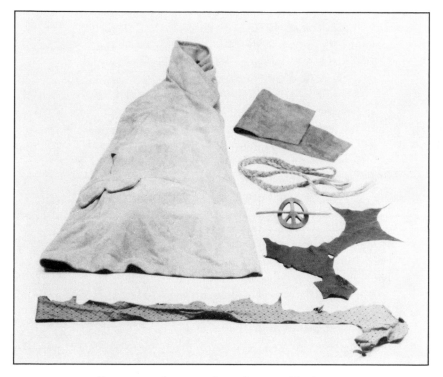

FEW KNOWN human cultures have used leather to a greater degree than the Aquarians. The "Indians," the aboriginal inhabitants of North Amerika, were a notable exception, and it is thought that the Aquarians were inspired by their example.

Leather offered great opportunities for the "self-expression" the Aquarians valued so highly, being suited to an extraordinary variety of techniques, decorative motifs and uses.

Analysis reveals that most Aquarian leather products were made from the skin of cows. This supports the findings of our nutritionists and agricultural specialists, who conjecture that the Aquarians were almost entirely vegetarian, except for the consumption of large numbers of Love Burgers made from ground beef.

HAND–THROWN POTTERY

CLAY, GLAZE, PAINT

DIMENSIONS: Assorted sizes

From the Hall of Shards Collection

HUNDREDS OF pieces of broken clay pottery were found scattered about the dig site, often near caches of macramé. Thanks to the tireless work and financial generosity of the Metroplex's chief sifter, Orchid Fonde, each of these fragments has now been cataloged, cleaned and mounted in the Metroplex's new Fonde Wing (also known as the Hall of Shards).

The sheer volume of shattered crockery is a sign that for the Aquarians the production of earthenware was a popular activity, but it is improbable that such vessels were actually intended to be used. The widespread availability of inexpensive, well-made plastic and glass containers would have made this highly impractical.

Aquarian pottery was more likely a sacrifice to the Aquarian god of creativity than anything else. Once a "craftsperson" had completed a piece of pottery, he or she would give it a long final look and then hurl it against the nearest wall. This practice was apparently the origin of the term "hand-thrown pottery."

WALL DECORATION

MANY WALL decorations of this type were found in Aquarian dwellings. Produced by unknown artists, they were generally cheap reproductions of now-lost masterpieces. The unique shapes and designs were intended to totally engage the eye and the consciousness of the viewer.

Unlike the rather static art of other cultures, many of the Aquarian artworks are kinetic. The example found here, which art historians are calling **Moving Dots,** is one of the best preserved. Fix your eye upon the center of the work and it appears to begin moving, ever so slightly at first and then more quickly, in circles, around and around and around and around. . . .

19

COMMUNAL LIVING

DIMENSIONS: Life Size

ARTIST: George Seagull

THE FOLLOWING is an excerpt from what was apparently the diary of a Berkeley Aquarian who had ventured to a rural outpost on a trading mission.

I was hitching up to Humboldt and no straights would pick me up, but like this fellow freak finally came along. We drove all night, toking the whole way, and he dropped me off right at the access road to Lodestar. He would have driven me all the way, but like the road was really rutted and that wouldn't have been cool for Camille, his pickup.

There was this sign saying NO VISITORS—WE ARE GOING THROUGH A HEAVY TIME RIGHT NOW AND CAN'T HANDLE ANY MORE PEOPLE TRYING OUT A NEW HEAD. *I just thought, Wow, I hope they got the crop in okay. Just as I came up to the main yurt some cat was ringing the gong for breakfast call. Everyone crawled out of their tepees and lean-tos, and like a lot of people were nude, but it was really cool. The pigs would never let you just be like that in Berkeley, man.*

Then this cat, Vishnu, and his old lady, Honeydew, came over and invited me to share the wealth of the land with everybody. There was a lot of rolled oats, but there was like only a quart of raw goat's milk for thirty people, so some cats decided to hitch into town to buy some pasteurized stuff and some doughnuts.

Honeydew was saying, "That whole trip they put food through in factories is fascist, but, hey, like you've got to use the system to expose the contradictions in the system, right?" Like, what they were using for bread right then was Honeydew's trust fund, which was blood money anyway, so why not turn it into something beautiful and peaceful, right?

Plus they had their cash crop, which is where I came in. They had a couple of lids all ready for me to sample. I mean, Vishnu and Honeydew and everyone else at Lodestar were beautiful people and everything, but there were still some cats who hadn't flashed on the whole brotherhood thing yet, and nobody wanted to get ripped off. A couple of tokes and I knew this was fantastic shit that was going to feed a lot of heads back in Berkeley for quite a while.

CHAPTER 2

AQUARIAN DRESS

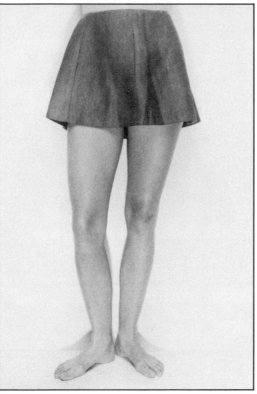

ITEM MOD67

MINIMAL SKIRT

65 PERCENT COTTON;
35 PERCENT POLYESTER

DIMENSIONS: Tiny

INSCRIPTION: "Machine Washable"

DUE TO its abbreviated nature, this article of clothing is thought to have been worn by female children-in the Aquarian community. Various examples were found throughout the dig site, leading some researchers to believe that the **Minimal Skirt** was a fundamental element of the Aquarian female child's wardrobe.

These garments were made from many materials, including the ubiquitous Aquarian "Blue Gene" fabric, and a petroleum-based polymer known as "plastic." "Plastic" apparently was used extensively during the Aquarian Age. Found in many products of the time, it was probably used as a material for children's clothing because it is easily washed. But the finest example in the exhibition is of the "solid color" variety (pictured here).

It is interesting that a noted celluloid entertainment of the Aquarians makes many references to a "plastics industry" as a source of financial opportunity. Many young Aquarians, it is assumed, worked in this industry.

ITEM 501
GARMENT WITH FLARED LEGS
CLOTH, DYE, METAL
DIMENSIONS: 32, 33L

THESE UNUSUAL trousers are an excellent example of the Aquarian desire for form to follow function. The pant legs were sewn so that the lower portion of the garment flared, allowing a great deal of freedom for the calf and foot. Examples have been found where the original flare was extended by ripping open the seams and sewing in an additional piece of cloth (usually brightly colored) to produce an even greater flare, and a startling visual effect as well. The flare at the bottom of the pants resembles a bell shape and researchers have jokingly referred to them as "bell-bottom" trousers.

Historians speculate that the original design for the "flared-leg" trouser was developed for British sailors to allow them to move about with acrobatic agility on the seas, when travel was in its infancy.* Evidently, the ground undulations experienced by the Aquarians of the Berkeley region were akin to the rolling waves of sea travel. This does not, however, explain how this type of clothing was developed centuries apart and halfway across the planet from its origin.

The name affixed to most examples of these pants—usually on an orange-colored tab—was **Levi.** This tab—in red as well as orange—was also attached to many other pieces of clothing found at the dig site. It is assumed Levi was the tradesman from nearby San Francisco who provided the Aquarians with much of their clothing.

*SOURCE: Ship & Shore's *High Seas and the British Navy*, 1842.

HEAVYWEIGHT COTTON, INSIGNIA
DIMENSIONS: One size fits all
INSCRIPTION: "Gilbert, US Army"

THE LARGE number of uniforms found at the dig led historians to conclude that the Aquarian standing army was a sizable one. Evidently, the Aquarian armed forces were extremely poorly equipped, since very few examples of military hardware were uncovered near the dig site.

The basic uniform jacket was either green or blue, depending on the branch of service. Patches that at one time must have signaled rank had been removed. (Did a mass demotion take place?) The uniform pants were worn loosely fitting and tucked into rugged black boots.

Not much is known about any engagements that the armed forces might have fought, but fragments

from songs and literature led researchers to believe that a small battle took place in what was known as *Ohio*, leaving four Aquarians dead. Other major engagements took place at a university in the East known as *Colombia*, and in the heart of the continent near *Chicago*. It seems that the largest number of battles took place on the Aquarians' home soil in Berkeley, culminating in what was known as *The Battle for People's Park*.

Apparently, the Aquarians were perplexed as to the reason for some of these actions, their battle song being "1–2–3 what are we fighting for?" The leader of the Aquarian armed forces is thought to have been one Commander Cody.

23

ITEM 10EEE
SANDALS
LEATHER, RUBBER, METAL BUCKLES
DIMENSIONS: 4″ × 12″
INSCRIPTION: > > > > >

THESE WERE the everyday footwear of the Aquarians, a testament to the health of a thriving leather industry. There were many different styles. One of the most common was secured to the foot by means of an ankle strap and was known as the "Roman" sandal. According to the lyric of a strangely atypical Aquarian song, these were not worn in Muskogee.

Muskogee is a settlement about which little else is known, except that it was a place where even "squares" could have a good time. Perhaps Muskogee was merely a mystical land where strange transformations of time, space and geometry took place; a place where reality was viewed entirely differently from the way the Aquarians saw it. An-

other explanation is that Muskogee was a real place whose inhabitants—the Okies—were offended by the fact that Roman sandals were sometimes referred to as "Jesus" sandals.

Another model was known as the "buffalo" sandal, and was one of the chief imports in the trade with India. The buffalo sandal was secured by leather loops that fit around the big and little toes. The soles of most sandals were made of leather, but the soles of the buffalo sandals were often made of rubber tire tread. This evidently was a feature preferred by members of the Cult of the Dead Heads, enamored as they were of their concept of "truckin'."

24

"KEEP YOUR HEAD TOGETHER" BAND

CLOTH, DYES, HUMAN AND CANINE HAIRS

DIMENSIONS: 6⁷/₈

AGENCY: Wild Thing

THE DISCOVERY of a number of headbands and other hair ornaments has led anthropologists to believe that many Aquarians wore their hair long. The widespread use of the headbands may explain the origin of one of the most popular Aquarian expressions, as the bands might be seen to be "keeping your head together" symbolically, or perhaps even literally, after a "bust" by the pigs.

The Aquarians lavished great attention on their hair, and one of their troubadors composed a song in its honor. They were urged to "grow it" and "show it," in whatever condition. For a brief time there was even the suggestion that this song become the national anthem of the Aquarians. Many individuals were particularly stirred by the soaring music accompanying the line that advised that hair which allowed the eyes to be seen was too short.

CHAPTER 3

SCIENCE AND TECHNOLOGY

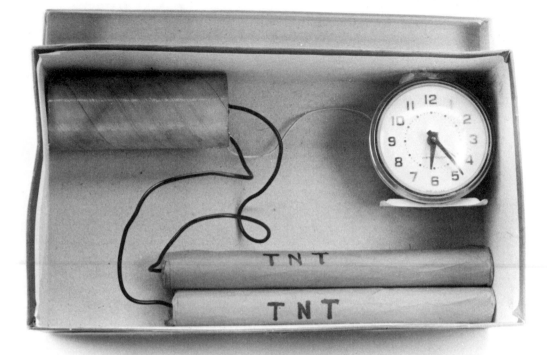

RECONSTRUCTION NO. 9

STRAWBERRY ALARM CLOCK

CHRONOMETER, WIRES, POWER CELL, DYNAMITE

DIMENSIONS: 4″ × 7″ × 12″

INSCRIPTION: "Pull to Set Alarm"

PIECES OF this reconstructed item—an ancient type of chronometer—were found scattered over a wide area of the dig site. Wires and batteries not normally associated with a chronometer were attached to some components. Each fragment bore traces of an ancient explosive called "dynamite."

The physical evidence suggests that the chronometer was used to trigger a rather substantial explosion. This at first baffled specialists in twentieth-century material culture, who were aware that the instrument's basic purpose was to awaken people in the morning. Given the Aquarians' bent for things communal, however, it is entirely possible that a single alarm clock, hooked up to a bomb, might be used to "wake up" an entire city.

The reconstruction pictured here was carried out according to drawings found in *The Anarchist's Cookbook.* Possibly this is the **Strawberry Alarm Clock** to which reference is made in other Aquarian literature.

ITEMS OP98, OP99

LIGHT SHOW
SPECIMEN SLIDES,
LAVA LAMP
GLASS, DYES, GOOP
DIMENSIONS: 7″ × 12″; 1½″ × 3″

THESE SPECIMEN slides have become one of the
great mysteries unearthed at the dig site. A thor-
ough analysis has been unable to detect any medical or scientific reason for the preparation of the
slides.

During one test, light was projected through
them. Then the slides were moved, whereupon bizarre, ever-changing shapes in bright hues were
cast upon the walls. Many researchers have com-
mented that watching the shapes causes disorien-
tation and that continued exposure induces a
hypnotic state, not wholly unpleasant.

One theory is that the slides were used in the de-
velopment of a device known as the "lava lamp,"
since there is some similarity between the lighting
effects of the slides and the lamp. Investigation
continues on solving the riddle of these devices.

ITEM G7
FOLK GUITAR

WOOD, NYLON, METAL, GLUE

DIMENSIONS: 15″ × 40″

INSCRIPTION: "C. F. Martin & Co., Est. 1833"

FROM SEVERAL sources we have learned that the standard Aquarian stringed instrument was the **Folk Guitar,** which was crafted by various tradesmen of the folk, for the folk and by the folk. The troubadors who were known for playing the Folk Guitar—Pete, Paul, Marie, Buffie, Saint, Marie, Judy, Joan, Joni, Donovan, Dylan and Arlo—were so popular among the Aquarians that they were known by their first names.

Many lesser troubadors also played the Folk Guitar at small gatherings or on the streets to serenade passersby. Then electricity was discovered by the Aquarians. The facts of this revolutionary discovery are no better known than the ones behind the discovery of fire by ancient cavemen, but the implications were no less profound.

New electrical instruments were connected to amplification devices that allowed the troubador to remain stationary rather than roam about to find an audience. The higher noise levels brought larger and larger crowds to hear the troubador play. Those who did not change with the times—for they were a-changin'—became moribund.

Unlike Folk Guitars, the new electrical instruments were sleek and brightly colored. Troubadors would often add designs to the original instrument to mark it as their own.

ELECTRICAL STRINGED INSTRUMENT
WOOD, PLASTIC, METAL
INSCRIPTION: "Gibson S-G"

The **Fender** Stratocaster

This versatile instrument was the favorite of troubadors during the later Aquarian Age. It could be played with the teeth as well as the hands, in front of the body or behind the neck, and was lubricated with flammable petroleum distillate.

Ludwig Drums

These drums became popular after they were introduced to the Aquarians through the music of the master percussionist **Ringo Richard Starkey,** a disciple of the long-ignored musical genius **Pete Best.**

Vox Amplification Systems

These "speakers," which "blew" amplified sounds to the gathered multitudes, enjoyed a brief reign in Aquarian lands but were replaced within a few short months by Fender's Amplification Systems.

Farfisa Organ

This was the electrified version of the high registers of a standard organ. Although reported to have lacked the resonance of the regular organ, it was louder. Most troubadors were accompanied by the Farfisa at one time or another, although it was quite limited in range and could play only four songs: "96 Tears," "Woolly Bully," "Light My Fire" and "Kind of a Drag."

All these instruments were to become central to the Aquarians' desire for music and decibels. They are thought to have undergone major changes in the decade following the 1960s and were entirely transformed by the 1980s.

The **Gibson S-G** Guitars

These combined the best elements of a Folk-type guitar with the added power of an electrical guitar. The many roaming troubador bands using Folk Guitars, who faced extinction due to the new electrical instruments, opted for the S-G. This did not compromise their desire for natural beauty but brought them heightened decibels and into the age of electrical music.

29

ITEM SX70

PUFF THE MAGIC DRAGON

PAPER, SILVER NITRATE

DIMENSIONS: 3″ × 5″

CREDIT: Courtesy Royal Academy

MANY CULTURES are known to have believed in creatures whose existence was rumored but never proved. There was the Loch Ness monster of the Land of the Scots, the Abdominal Snowman of the Hi-MAL-yas, and especially **Puff the Magic Dragon** of the Aquarians.

The dragon was thought to reside in the land of *Honilee*, although the exact location of *Honilee* is not known and is not shown on any existing maps of Aquarian lands. An Aquarian song reveals, however, that Puff lived "by the sea"—which sea remains a mystery.

An Aquarian named Jackie Paper reportedly sighted Puff and became great friends with the dragon. As Jackie grew older his contact with Puff lessened until "one gray night" he ceased seeing the dragon at all. The reason for the end of this beautiful friendship belongs to history.

The Royal Academy has twice mounted expeditions to former Aquarian lands rumored to be the habitat of Puff the Magic Dragon. During one of these expeditions the above photograph was taken of a creature thought to be Puff, although this has never been verified.

RITUAL DRUG ROULETTE CASE

PLASTIC, TRACE ELEMENTS
DIMENSIONS: 3″ × 4″
INSCRIPTION: "Dial-A-Pack"

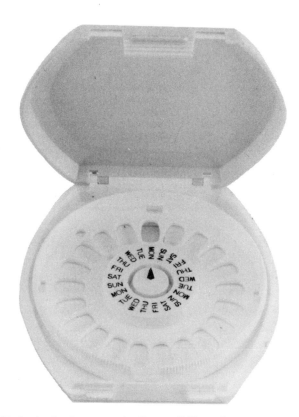

THIS INGENIOUS molded plastic "one-per-day" container held a supply of ritual drugs. Interestingly, the number of chambers corresponds to the days of the month in the primeval Aquarian Lunar Calendar.

One chamber contained a peyote seed whose hallucinogenic properties were first discovered accidentally by agricultural specialists. Another bore traces of a crude derivative of the common grain mold ergot. When ingested the substance induced a fantastic mental "journey" during which our volunteers claimed to be able to "taste" colors and "see" music.

Still another compartment held a powdered extract of the coca plant. The white dust produced numbness of the gums when taken orally. Yet when a researcher inhaled it through the nose, he became very active, talkative and amorous.

Pharmacologists were perplexed, however, to discover several substances within the case whose effect was unclear. These included baked powdered-banana peel; salicylic acid ("aspirin"); and a tablet composed mainly of human female hormones, which induced heart attacks, strokes and other vascular disorders in laboratory animals.

STEAM ENGINE

GLASS, RUBBER, WATER
SCALE: 1:1000
INSCRIPTION: "Bong-zai"

THIS WAS apparently a scale model for a giant engine that would have captured heat from deep inside the Earth and used it to generate electricity. A long tube would be inserted into one of the many faults in the Berkeley area. The heat rising through the tube would convert the water in the engine's central chamber into steam. The steam would be released through another tube and used to drive a turbine that would generate electricity.

Evidently, large-scale testing of the device was conducted using heat produced by burning hemp. This made excellent sense, considering the plant's widespread availability. Many variations of the model pictured here were discovered, all bearing the telltale residue of the Aquarians' staple crop.

Unfortunately, the Aquarians never built a full-scale version of their ingenious steam engine. The remains of a somewhat similar device, however, were found at Devil's Canyon, a few hundred miles south of Berkeley. For unknown reasons, the ruins were highly radioactive. Although built upon a fault line that later became the starting point of an earthquake which destroyed it, this plant bears only a superficial resemblance to the Aquarian invention.

HIGHLIGHTS
OF THE EXHIBITION

ITEMS T1, T2, T3
T-SHAPED GARMENT
100 PERCENT COTTON, DYES
DIMENSIONS: Small, Medium,
Large, X-Large

INSCRIPTION:
"Colors may run when washed"

IT IS believed that the many colors, designs and slogans that decorated these unisex garments were indicative of social status and work roles within the Aquarian community.

For example, the plain, pocketed **"T-shirt"** (especially in the darker colors) was most likely the customary garb of low-level Aquarian workers, such as cooks, pottery kiln operators or field hands.

Some garments bore commercial or political slogans and were probably worn by individuals employed specifically to let others know "what was going down." Besides the slogans affixed to the garments pictured here, others included WAR IS UNHEALTHY FOR CHILDREN AND OTHER LIVING THINGS, TODAY IS THE FIRST DAY OF THE REST OF YOUR LIFE, GIVE A DAMN, FREAK FREELY, QUESTION AUTHORITY, LSD DID THIS TO ME, and DICK NIXON BEFORE HE DICKS YOU.

The most elaborate of the garments, often featuring dye coloring, were undoubtedly favored by Aquarian dignitaries, such as cult leaders, festival promoters and leading ritual-drug merchants. Combined with Aquarian jewelry—crude, colorful beads or glowing turquoise stones set in hand-worked silver rings, bracelets and earrings—these garments must have produced an effect of great splendor.

ITEM 502
TAPESTRY PANTS AND DETAIL
CLOTH, DYE, METAL, LEATHER, CANVAS, COLORED THREAD, MINIATURE FLAGS
DIMENSIONS: Uncertain due to decomposition

ART HISTORIANS were boggled by the discovery of a series of tapestries that for ornateness and ambition rival the Bayeux Tapestry of ancient European Earth culture. These remarkable, wearable, moving tapestries show a degree of sophistication and attention to detail not found in other Aquarian art forms.

When worn, the tapestry would reveal a blend of color and texture that would make an "impressionistic" statement. Each pair of pants (some with a higher content of embroidery than others) was hand-sewn with precision. Each design motif or block of color was perfectly meshed to another.

The visual effect upon first viewing a pair of "tapestry pants" is moving. The combined effect of many of the tapestries placed side to side must have been a truly transcendental experience.

FRINGED LEATHER JACKET

ANIMAL SKIN, SYNTHETIC FIBER, CLOTH, METAL
DIMENSIONS: 3'6" × 4'8"
INSCRIPTION: "Dry Clean Only"

THIS ITEM was at first believed to have been improperly attributed to the 1960s, since similar garments were in common use among the "cowboys" of the North Amerikan West in the nineteenth century. However, argon dating has now determined that it is indeed of 1960s manufacture.

We know that the cowboy was associated in Aquarian culture with romantic notions of freedom. Perhaps the Aquarians were making a poignant attempt to inject this quality into their own lives. Or possibly they were harking back to the even more distant origins of the fringed jacket—to the aboriginal inhabitants of the North Amerikan Plains, the "Indians."

This is a more plausible theory, since it is believed that the Aquarians identified closely with the Indians. The Aquarians derived their drug rituals, which they believed to have religious significance, directly from surviving aboriginal cultures. Many of these rituals were passed on to the Aquarians by Carlos Castaneda, a disciple of the noted "medicine man" Don Juan. One of the latter's most important teachings was how to avoid being turned into a dog or a crow.

ITEM 69
LOVE BEADS
LEATHER, CERAMIC BEADS
DIMENSIONS: Expandable

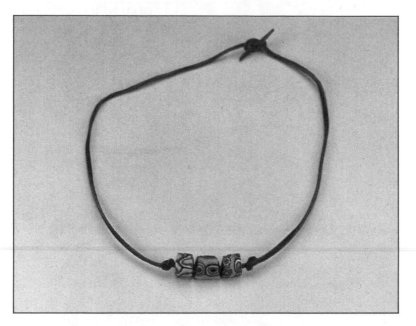

IF AN Aquarian could own just one piece of jewelry, it would almost certainly be **Love Beads.** Love Beads could be made from practically any durable material, from plastic to papier-mâché to macaroni, and were generally brilliantly colored.

A strand might hold anywhere from a single bead to dozens, leading anthropologists to conclude that Love Beads were not purely decorative in function. It is now believed that they also offer important clues to sexual behavior, with the number of beads corresponding to the number of an Aquarian's lovers. It is significant that the strands were simply strung and easily expandable. The color and design of the beads are thought to have been carefully coded to indicate how good a lover had been.

Two of the most popular materials for stringing beads were cotton string and leather cord. It is not known whether there was any significance in the choice of material, although perhaps it had something to do with the sexual preferences of the wearer.

THE AQUARIAN NAVY

METAL, PAINT
SCALE: 1:50
ARTIST: Peter Maximum

THE EXISTENCE of an Aquarian navy is documented in many famous Aquarian songs—"Yellow Submarine" and "Wooden Ships," to name just two. However, the navy's sailing routes and strategic value, if any, are difficult to ascertain.

What is known is that the Aquarians established sea trade with several other Earth cultures. Perhaps wooden ships and the sophisticated **Peter Maximum**-designed yellow submarine were the chief vessels of this trade.

Like the famous ocean-going ships **Nina, Pinta** and **Santa Maria**—whose captain is thought to have discovered the continent eventually inhabited by the Aquarians—the **Sloop John B.** ventured to the exotic Carob Ocean on a mission of exploration and trade. During the voyage, the crew was beset with many trials and tribulations, which caused them to lament for their homeland.

"IF YOU'RE GOING TO SAN FRANCISCO"

STYLING: Mr. Rob

PROPS: Flowers 'R' Fun

AGENCY: That Girl

THE PLEASANT little ditty "If You're Going to San Francisco" was a tribute to the successful "summer of love" when Aquarians ceased all ordinary enterprises to engage in mass cultural bliss. The population explosion in the Berkeley/San Francisco Bay area the following year was thought to have been caused by this "summer of love."

The song advises that those traveling to San Francisco would meet very nice people. Furthermore, it suggests that when in San Francisco one should do as the San Franciscans do, and wear flowers in one's hair. What type of flower is not mentioned in the song. The custom, in any case, was a charming one.

THE AQUARIAN ENTREPRENEUR

SILVER, TURQUOISE, SUGAR CUBES
DIMENSIONS: 3″ × 4″; Bite Size
INSCRIPTION: "Motherlode Crafts, N.M."

IT IS not recorded which brave Aquarian explorer first ventured into the wilds of New Mexico. But like other great explorers whose discovery of a new substance (Marco Polo and his silk, Sir Walter Raleigh and his tobacco) changed history, this bold Aquarian brought back a unique product heretofore unknown to the Aquarians: the combination of silver and turquoise.

At the same time, in an unrelated discovery, a young Aquarian alchemist known as Owsley created a powerful ritual drug that would become the most taken, talked about and revered of all the ritual drugs: the sugar cube. By what means this chemical genius formed the particles of sugar into a perfect cube is not known, but the effects of the sugar cube on the Aquarian population were mind blowing.

The importance of these two discoveries is that they gave rise to an independent Aquarian economy which did not exist until this time. Prior to these discoveries, Aquarians were forced to live on the largesse of the rival Amerikans for food and shelter. The Aquarians thought the Amerikans were "ripping them off" and leaped at the chance to turn the tables.

During the "summer of love," Aquarian entrepreneurs flooded the streets of their homeland with hastily franchised silver and turquoise stands. Thousands of sugar cubes were manufactured in expectation of the demand that would be brought about by the influx of tourists for that summer promotion. "Underground" newspapers were created to inform tourists of the doings in Aquarian society, and they too became successful enterprises.

The success of these new industries and the resultant infusion of capital made it possible for the Aquarians to further expand their infant economy into other areas of commerce, such as leather goods, pottery and artworks. The fate of the forward-thinking Owsley is not known, but he is rumored to have become a very rich man, living the rest of his life in self-imposed anonymity.

"ROACH" CLIPS

VARIOUS METALS, BEADS

DIMENSIONS: Easily concealed

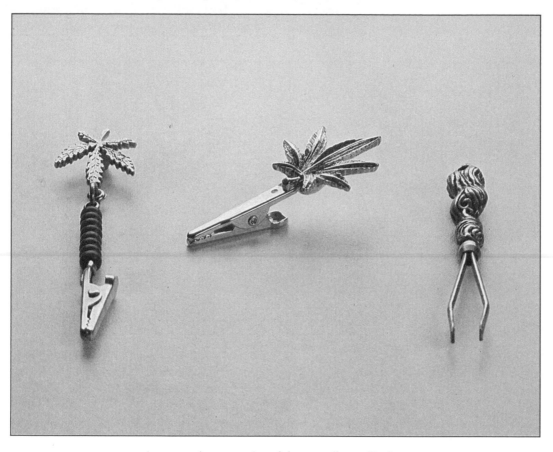

AN EARLY interpretation of these small metallic devices supposed that during the great cockroach epidemics of the twentieth century, in which billions of the insects infested the cities of North Amerika, the clips were somehow used to pin the creatures down in order to exterminate them. However, this interpretation has since fallen into discredit.

A more plausible hypothesis is that the Aquarians used the clips to fasten a live "roach" (or facsimile) to a piece of clothing to signify that the wearer was in spiritual harmony with the cosmos. The Aquarians, like other ancient human cultures, particularly the Egyptians, believed the cockroach to be a sacred beast that had found favor with the gods and would be granted immortality.

CHAPTER 4

THE FINE ARTS

DIORAMA 3
THE GREAT FLOOD
SCALE: 1:25
ARTIST: Kristo

MUCH OF Aquarian history was committed to song, in keeping with the traditions of many cultures throughout the ages. The early history of the Aquarians was of special interest to our researchers, and the song fragment "The Times They Are A-Changin' " recounts the story of the great flood that forced the Aquarians to migrate to the Berkeley Basin.

Most ancient cultures have a myth of a great flood, which destroys all that went before and spares only the righteous. The individuals who survive the flood become the "chosen people." The Aquarians obviously thought of themselves in this way. Their song advises that they should begin swimming or they would sink "like a stone," and evidently they managed to save themselves.

The exact location of the Aquarian great flood is unknown. Possibly the reference is to the overflowing of the banks of the Hudson River, since many early Aquarians came from the land of the Green Village, which was located near this river. All that is known of the Green Village is that its principal products were coffees prepared in exotic ways, which were sipped by the populace in sidewalk cafés both day and night.

DIORAMA 4
STREET BATTLE
SCALE: Life Size
ARTIST: Dwayne Hansom
THEME SONG:
"For What It's Worth"

THIS SONG was written and performed by a band of troubadors called Buffalo Springfield (an excellent example of the Aquarian love of naming themselves in honor of the aboriginal inhabitants of North Amerika). It is a commemoration of one of the great battles of the Aquarians, although which one is not known.

The song tells of a large engagement in an unknown town on a very hot day when a thousand Aquarians took to the streets. In what must have been a stirring sight for any Aquarian patriot, they sang songs and carried signs proclaiming HOORAY for the Aquarians.

The song goes on to describe the circumstances that led up to the battle, the paranoia which gripped the Aquarians and their fear of stepping out of line in the face of the enemy. Members of Buffalo Springfield would later chronicle other great Aquarian battles such as *Ohio* and *Chicago*.

SGT. PEPPER
CANVAS, OIL PAINT
DIMENSIONS: 2′ × 3′
SELF-PORTRAIT

"LUCY IN the Sky with Diamonds" is perhaps the finest example of lyric poetry found in Aquarian culture. A mystical tale on the order of the great poem *Kubla Khan*, its author, Sgt. Pepper, apparently was under the influence of some type of ritualistic drug or had just returned from a long trip to a faraway land.

The song tells of a search for a woman (not unlike the Lady of the Lake of Arthurian legend) who has "kaleidoscope" eyes. The author follows her to the land of "rocking horse people" and incredibly large flowers. He then pursues her in a "newspaper taxi" to a train station, where he discovers her at the "turnstile."

Like Coleridge's verse, the song seems to end upon the poet's awakening from a dream with no resolution, yet his trip seems to have been worthwhile. The title is thought to be a code of some kind. This belief has prompted musicologists to call upon the services of famous cryptologist Ann O. Graham in an attempt to unravel the full meaning of "Lucy in the Sky with Diamonds."

43

SPACE PROGRAM

DETERMINATION AND KNOW-HOW
DIMENSIONS: 30,000 pounds of thrust
PROGRAM MOTTO: "Let's Get High"

"EIGHT MILES HIGH" is thought to have been the theme song for the Aquarian space program. Judging from the limited technology in evidence at the dig site, the program must have been in its infancy. The troubadors who performed this song were appropriately called **The Birds.**

"Eight Miles High" chronicles the imaginary first trip into outer space and the strange things the Aquarians expected to find when they would "touch down" there. Although the Aquarians had a fervent love of space, studied it in their astrology, wanted to be "given space" and referred to "getting high" extensively in their literature, there is no proof they were ever able to successfully launch their space program.

THE AQUARIANS had great dreams for the future, as evidenced by this celluloid entertainment. Although their space program was fledgling at best, they created a "moving picture," which showed the early history of the Earth and a voyage into the cosmos by the intrepid Aquarian space travelers Hal and Dave.

The Aquarians also had an uncanny knowledge about things they should have been ignorant of—witness their highly accurate description in *2001* of the **Monolith,** which was until recently housed on Gamma Delta 2 but in the 1960s was located on the satellite moon Ribbit 5. *2001* also gave a precise prediction of the dangers of robot machines, which were realized in our own *Techno War 1* on the planet *Zincbar.*

RECONSTRUCTION HAL2001

2001: A SPACE ODYSSEY

PLASTIC, SILICON CHIPS, VARIOUS METALS

DIMENSIONS: Bigger than a PC, smaller than a Univac

AUDIO FRAGMENT: "I'm sorry, Dave. I can't do that, Dave."

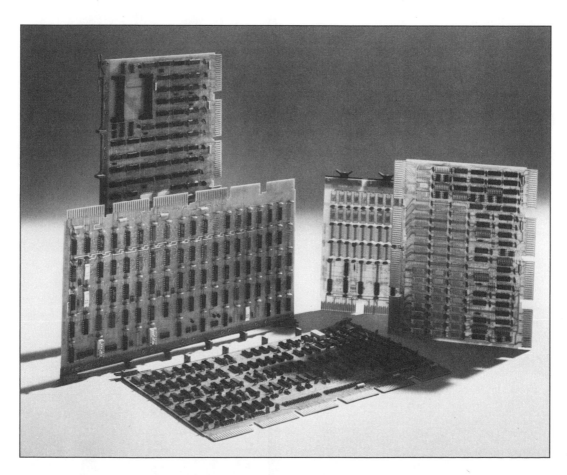

REEFER MADNESS

ACAPULCO GOLD, SEEDS, STEMS,
PIPE, PAPER

SCALE: Life Size

AUDIO FRAGMENT: "Why do you think
they call it dope?"

IT SEEMS that this celluloid reel was actually a
medical film intended to educate the Aquarians
about the dangers of ingesting or inhaling large
quantities of the smoke of their beloved hemp, including lewd behavior and madness. It is interesting to note that one of the staples of Aquarian
society was also possibly its downfall.

From the literature of the time, we know that
those who controlled the hemp strings were not ea-
ger to have Aquarian society influenced by this celluloid, and launched a smear campaign that
ridiculed the reel's conclusions.

MAYFIELD, USA

WOOD, TAR, GRASS
SCALE: 21″ Diagonal
ARTIST: Levitt Towne

DURING THEIR formative years, the Aquarians spent many hours a day watching a primitive video device called **The Tube.** Apparently, The Tube was used to indoctrinate youngsters with the fundamental myths and fantasies of Aquarian culture.

Perhaps the most important of all the "shows" appearing on The Tube was one featuring a small boy known as "The Beaver" or "The Beave." The Beaver lived in a clean, attractive "home" on a tree-shaded street in **Mayfield, USA.** His parents never had disagreements, never struck their children and always looked dressed up. **"Mom/June"** spent her days baking cookies for The Beaver and his friends, while **"Dad/Ward"** occupied himself with what was mysteriously referred to as a "job." Occasionally, The Beaver would run into problems at home or school, but nothing that couldn't be solved by the end of the "show."

Surely Mayfield was the Eden of the Aquarians, the mythical time and place that all cultures invent for themselves, the paradise that existed before The Fall. Best of all, life there was eternal, for no one ever seemed to die in Mayfield; they just went into "syndication."

47

GILLIGAN'S ISLAND
PAPER, INK, SEA WATER, PAPAYA JUICE
DIMENSIONS: 18″ × 24″

Curator's Note: Only known map of otherwise
uncharted desert isle

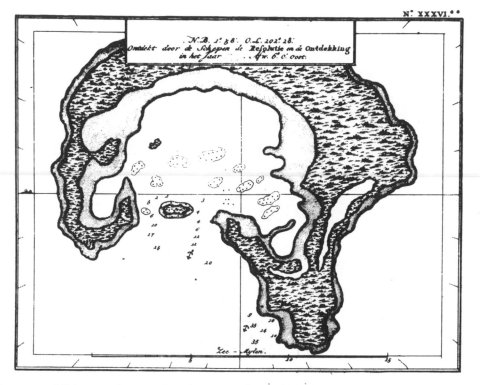

If Mayfield, USA, was the paradise that had been lost to the Aquarians, **Gilligan's Island** represented the one that might be found again.

On the uncharted desert isle were to be found the key personnel needed to establish a self-sufficient and well-rounded society. There was Gilligan (the village idiot), the Skipper too (the natural leader), the Millionaire (capital) and his wife (conspicuous consumption), the Movie Star (fertility), the Professor (learning) and Mary Ann (good clean fun).

Gilligan's Island is thought to have been an inspiration to the founders of the communal rural outposts of the Aquarians. In both locales, work was assigned according to the abilities of the members, although the majority of time was spent extricating them from "humorous" situations.

In only one respect was the society of Gilligan's Island less than idyllic. Apparently, something in the air or water made procreation impossible, since no children were born to Ginger or Mary Ann during the many long seasons the castaways were marooned on the island.

Since the Gilligan's Island community could not perpetuate itself, it had to be rescued or perish. Alas, however, even being rescued could not save it. The society could not sustain itself "back on the mainland" and all of the members "went their separate ways."

SATURDAY MORNING CARTOONS

CELLULOID, IMAGINATION, PLIABLE YOUNG MINDS

RUNNING TIME: 30 minutes with commercials

AUDIO FRAGMENT: "We'll be right back after a brief word from our sponsor."

LIKE THE morality plays of the Middle Ages, the **Saturday Morning Cartoons** of the Aquarians both entertained and instructed. Perhaps a closer comparison would be to the fables of Aesop, since the main characters of most of the cartoons were animals.

The characters represented all social classes, from the "aristocat" Top Cat to middle-class moralist Jiminy Cricket to the asocial Daffy Duck. Virtually all occupational areas were represented as well, including law enforcement (Quick Draw McGraw), education (Mr. Peabody), marriage counseling (Mickey and Minnie Mouse), counter-intelligence (Rocky and Bullwinkle) and public speaking (Donald Duck).

Each of these characters had his ardent fans among the Aquarians, but the most popular of all were The Roadrunner and his archenemy, Wiley E. Coyote. Coyote, backed by the military-industrial complex represented by *Acme Products*, developed ingenious schemes for making a meal of The Roadrunner. Yet his happy-go-lucky, bird-brained foe always managed to avoid capture and to cause Coyote's plans to backfire. The Roadrunner is of interest to physicists as well as cultural historians for he could apparently accelerate from a standing start to supersonic speeds in an interval too brief to be measured by science. Interestingly, the Saturday Morning Cartoons were sometimes interrupted by attempted launchings of the Aquarian space program.

For unknown reasons, the cartoons were almost always viewed under the influence of ritual drugs. Perhaps the Aquarians believed that the "visions" presented by the cartoons would be more impressive under these circumstances.

RECONSTRUCTION 3
"KEEP ON TRUCKIN'"
METAL, CHROME, RUBBER, DIESEL FUEL
DIMENSIONS: 10-4
ARTIST: R. Crumb

CRUMB IS thought to have been one of the greatest of Aquarian painters, although little of his work survived the great undulations of the 1960s. He was revered by the populace, the troubadors, members of the Cult of the Dead Heads and the chief newspapers of the day, from the *Berkeley Barb* to the *Chicago Seed*. Like many other immortal artists, he was preoccupied with a single great theme—"truckin"—which recurs again and again in his work.

CHAPTER 5

THE LITERATURE OF THE AQUARIANS

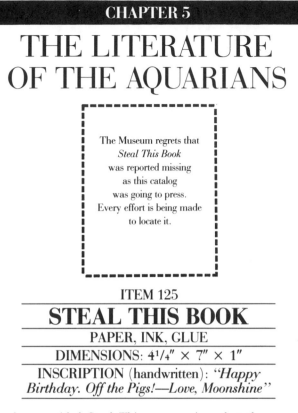

The Museum regrets that
Steal This Book
was reported missing
as this catalog
was going to press.
Every effort is being made
to locate it.

ITEM 125

STEAL THIS BOOK

PAPER, INK, GLUE

DIMENSIONS: 4¹/₄″ × 7″ × 1″

INSCRIPTION (handwritten): *"Happy Birthday. Off the Pigs!—Love, Moonshine"*

THE DISCOVERY of a volume entitled *Steal This Book* was particularly fascinating for researchers called in from the University of Roman à Clef. The volume had sustained serious water damage and was found encased in a porcelain receptacle. Both the cover and title page were clearly marked "Steal This Book," and small, reconstructed fragments of the jacket reveal what is apparently the image of a wild–haired man.

The researchers discounted the explanations presented by the distinguished etymologist H. Word Smith that the use of the word "steal" was actually wordplay based on the 1897 edition of the *Encyclopedia of Sport*, which defines "steal" as "a long putt unexpectedly holed," leading Smith to read the title *Putt This Book*.

Linguists were forced to confront the startling fact that the apparent intention of the author was to invite the potential owner of the book to remove it from commercial premises without paying for it.

The discovery of *Steal This Book* raises many more questions than it answers. Were its contents so precious that they must be obtained by any means, including stealing? Was it an instructional manual that taught Aquarians how to steal books in general, and possibly even other goods? Were the Aquarians a group so cut off from the general culture that money which could have been used to purchase books was not available to them?

Unless the volume can somehow be restored and the text explicated, these questions may never be answered. It is known, however, that the author, Abigail Hoffman, was a member of a political party known as "the Yippies," of which little is known.

Professor Smith is currently working to decipher the meaning of the name. One theory he has put forward is that "Yippie" is a sort of double pun, since it is a longer form of the nineteenth-century English word "yip" (archaic long before the 1960s), which means "to cheep like a newly born bird." He points out that "cheep" may be a play on the popular 1960s word "cheap," suggesting the real reason a Yippie would "steal" a book.

The Gestalt Prayer

I do my thing, and you do your thing.
I am not in this world to live up to your expec-
    tations
And you are not in this world to live up to mine.
You are you, and I am I,
And if by chance, we find each other, it's beautiful.
If not, it can't be helped.

Frich Perls.

ONLY A few complete Aquarian poems were unearthed at the Berkeley site. Undoubtedly highly revered texts, they were printed on large paper scrolls and probably owe their survival to the fact that they were rolled up inside a sealed cylindrical plastic tube.

One piece of verse, attributed to a Frederick S. Perls, is reproduced here. The great mystery of this text is concealed within the word "thing." What was the "thing" the Aquarians were so keen on doing? What was the reason for doing it? How did they know when they found it?

If only literary historians, linguists, sociologists or other specialists could answer these questions, our understanding of Aquarian culture would be advanced far past its present state. In any case, such was the wisdom of Perls available to the Aquarians.

AQUARIAN POETRY II

PAPER, INK

DIMENSIONS: 12″ × 24″

INSCRIPTION (handwritten): *"Dad, when you read this I hope you can understand where I'm coming from.—Your Son"*

I Know that you Believe you Understand what you Think I said, But, I am not Sure you Realize that what you heard is not what I meant.

STEFFEN & GAINES, INC. ©1972 Printed in U.S.A.   P.O. BOX 785 - SAUSALITO, CALIFORNIA 94965

THIS BRIEF example of Aquarian verse set linguists to scratching their heads in perplexity. "There are so many levels of uncertainty here," explained one, "that we have no clear idea what this verse means, but it is obviously very profound. The tone is plaintive, even whining, and seems to reflect a desperate desire on the part of the narrator to make himself understood. This is surely too simple an interpretation, however, for in that case he would have used plain English."

Scholars of religious thought offered the view that the verse was not unlike a Zen Buddhist koan, an insoluble riddle that would either lead a person to enlightenment or drive him crazy. This perspective is supported by other evidence of the influence of Asian cultures upon the Aquarians.

Still other analysts theorized that the poem was an experimental work designed to stretch the capacities of the Aquarian dialect, Hipenglish, to their limits and beyond.

AQUARIAN POETRY III

PARCHMENT, INK

DIMENSIONS: 12″ × 18″

INSCRIPTION (handwritten): *"Krishna. You know they found this written on a church door centuries ago. Beautiful.—Love, Rama"*

> *Go placidly amid the noise & haste,*
> *& remember what peace there may be in silence…*
>
> *You are a child of the universe,*
> *no less than the trees & the stars; you have a right*
> *to be here.*
>
> *with all its sham, drudgery and broken dreams,*
> *it is still a beautiful world…*
>
> *—Anonymous*

LITERARY HISTORIANS read these fragments of verse as fairly direct commentary upon conditions in Aquarian society.

In a community so enamored of loud music, what advice could be more appropriate than "go placidly amid the noise & haste," and especially "remember what peace there may be silence."

Since Aquarian men and women lived communally and "got it on" with many partners, the male parentage of children must often have been called into question. At least a youngster could always be told, "You are a child of the universe."

Finally, when the ritual drugs turned out to have been "cut," when a weary Aquarian just couldn't "handle" another tribal gathering, when the "revolution" foretold in Aquarian story and song never came, it must have been soothing to be told, "It is still a beautiful world."

WE ARE THE PEOPLE OUR PARENTS WARNED US AGAINST

PAPER, INK, GLUE

DIMENSIONS: 4¼" × 7" × 1"

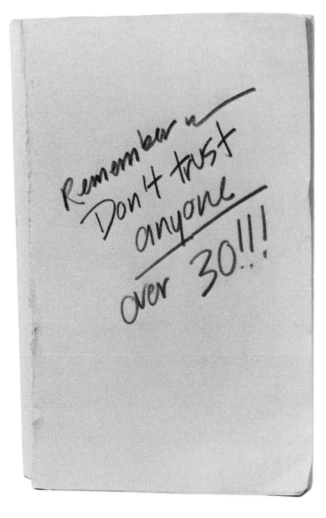

THIS WAS apparently an Aquarian father's tome, addressed to his son or daughter. It hints at the dark side of Aquarian culture—the eradication of all those over the age of thirty during the establishment of the Aquarian Age.

As with the other ritualistic cultures that have been studied over the ages (especially those which sacrificed virgins; or, more to the point, the cannibals), it is not for us to judge a civilization of which we know so little. Perhaps a lack of food or a natural disaster made it necessary for all the feeble to be destroyed so that Aquarian society would survive. Did the Spartans not leave sickly children on the mountainside to die so as to keep the race strong and pure?

Undoubtedly, the life-span of the Aquarians was much shorter than ours is now. Perhaps the elimination of the adults was simply a matter of a mass "mercy killing."

Much of the book was illegible, but what is evident is that the Aquarians lived in fear that their children would one day grow up and eradicate everyone over the age of thirty as they themselves had. Perhaps this book was an effort to explain their actions and to prevent a recurrence of what must have been for Aquarians a terrible necessity.   55

ITEM 137

ON THE ROAD

PAPER, INK, GLUE

DIMENSIONS: 4¼″ × 7″ × 1″

INSCRIPTION (handwritten): *"What a long strange trip it's been.—Neal"*

THE FOLLOWING essay is provided by the leading literary critic in the field of Aquarian literature, author of the forthcoming *Waterwords: The Writings of the Aquarians*, B. Nick.

I got hip to this Aquarian writer, Jack, Jack Kerouac, when this digger from the gig out at Berkeley laid the book on me and I wasn't really in the mood to read it after three days of riding from bar to bar in Cosmic City with this waitress and her sister looking for some cat who supposedly could play the old 1960s "blues music" and I just wanted to find this cat and after two days and the waitress is sitting next to me and her sister is out in the backseat and I didn't even remember my lady was at home waiting for me and a whole lot of mail piled up, but I read this Kerouac anyway. This cat was gone.

Dig this. It's about this cat who finds this con who wants to live so hard he is constantly on the make, for food, for women, for cars. Man, for cars but not to keep them but to take them out and drive them hard and if they get trashed you get another one, a Cadillac or a Hudson (man, I hear those Hudsons could move like balling a jack) and they go across country and they just live. This guy was like an Aquarian Marco Polo, this Jack, this father we never had, this mind so sharp and keen and real, *really* real *for his time and anytime.*

When I finished this thing and the lady wasn't too interested in banging since I hadn't been around for a few days and she was going to let me know, I grabbed the digger's find and took off for a few experiences of my own and to just let it happen to me because you can read and write about reading and everything but you can't be sure about anything or anybody except it gets old and the only thing to do is go out and try to find the origins of life-bliss as only a writer like Jack, Jack Kerouac, could do it. I dug it.

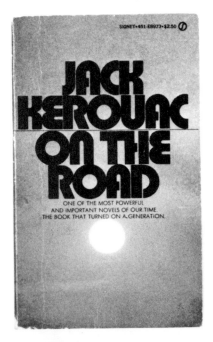

56

THE WHOLE EARTH CATALOG

RECYCLED PAPER, VEGETABLE-BASED INK, BIODEGRADABLE GLUE
DIMENSIONS: 11″ × 14½″ × 1½″
INSCRIPTION: "access to tools"

ONE STEWART BRAND is credited with authoring a massive catalog that purported to be a source book of objects, services and advice Aquarians could acquire.

Literary historians have determined that this catalog is in all likelihood a hoax of the magnitude of two other notorious twentieth-century ruses: Clifford Irving's fabrication of Howard Hughes's autobiography, and the forged diaries of the infamous madman Adolf Hitler.

The speculation is that *The Whole Earth Catalog* was created as a parody of the Aquarians' love of catalogs of all kinds and descriptions. A careful cross-checking of the various goods and services in the catalog with what is known of the culture of the time leads researchers to conclude that most entries are too farfetched to be believed. They did concede that it took a great deal of creativity and imagination to produce the catalog.

QUOTATIONS FROM CHAIRMAN MOUSEY DUNG

DIMENSIONS: $2^3/_4'' \times 3^1/_2''$
INSCRIPTION: "WORKERS OF ALL COUNTRIES, UNITE!"

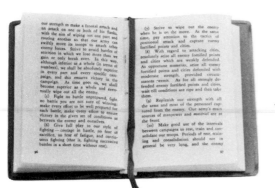

FRAGMENTS OF a little red book entitled *Quotations from Chairman Mousey Dung* outline certain military "principles of operation." Historical evidence indicates that the Aquarians adopted these principles wholeheartedly in their campaigns against the Amerikans.

. . . do not make holding or seizing a city or place our main objective. . . . Often a city or place can be held or seized for good only after it has changed hands a number of times.

Though the Aquarians had established beachheads in most of the giant megalopolises of North Amerika (the Green Village on the East Coast, Hateashbury in San Francisco), the populations of these areas were very much in flux, with new recruits arriving at all times and "burned-out" veterans moving on. Sometimes, these settlements would be abandoned entirely, with residents retreating to another part of the same city or to an entirely new locale.

In every battle, concentrate an absolutely superior force (two, three, four and sometimes even five and six times the enemy's strength), encircle the enemy forces completely, strive to wipe them out thoroughly and do not let any escape through the net.

This principle immediately recalls the battles of Chicago and the Pentagon.

Replenish our strength with all the arms and most of the personnel captured from the enemy.

The Aquarians, basically peaceful, relied more on the size of their forces than on weapons. They did, however, recruit extensively among the Amerikans. They even tried to rally Amerikan soldiers to their side by placing flowers in their gun barrels.

Make good use of the intervals between campaigns to rest, train and consolidate our troops.

The Aquarians followed this principle faithfully. However:

Periods of rest, training and consolidation should not in general be very long. . . .

This corollary was mysteriously ignored.

RECONSTRUCTION 10
MOBY GRAPE
DIMENSIONS: Thought to have been a
book of enormous size
ARTIST: Herbie Buchbinder

LIKE MANY other Aquarian troubadors, the San Francisco group **Moby Grape** is thought to have derived its name from a literary source. Indeed, many scholars believe *Moby Grape* is the great lost novel of the Aquarians. The subject recently became the focus of a heated debate at the Fourth Universal Symposium of Hard-to-Understand Literature (USHTUL for short).

After a spirited discussion of *Finnegans Wake* and a tepid recital of an easily forgotten paper on the complexity of plot in *Love Story*, scholars addressed the question of the actual existence of the lost *Moby Grape*. Professor François Explicateur insisted that he has found many references in the literature of now-defunct cultures to a novel about the fanatical Captain Ahab, who pursues a giant champagne grape through the wilds of the area north of the Aquarians' homeland. To which USHTUL chairman Professor Pan Dantic retorted, "Tish!"

Undeterred by the shouts of other experts, Explicateur continued his story of the grape, now floating out to sea with the one-legged captain madly rowing after it, assisted by his faithful companion Wigwag. The symposium was called to order after Explicateur was forcibly restrained.

BERKELEY BARB
PAPER, INK, AMMONIA, CLAY
DIMENSIONS: 12″ × 14″

A COPY of the great daily newspaper of the Aquarians was found in a plastic tray inscribed with the cryptic message "Kitti Rest Stop," its pages covered by clay saturated with ammonia. This may explain the paper's survival through the ages.

The *Barb* was a journal that served the needs of its readers well. Biting political articles and detailed accounts of transgressions against the oppressed Aquarians filled the opening pages. Listings of rides to other parts of Woodstock Nation as well as free educational opportunities were cataloged. The paper also informed Aquarians of forthcoming festivals and of valuable self-defense techniques to be used if an Aquarian was attacked by a hostile animal (usually a pig) or an invader from Amerika.

Perhaps the most widely read feature of the paper was the "Personals" column. The following is one example of how it was used: "Moondog—You were the dude with the red bandanna and the silver front tooth. We met while tripping in Golden Gate Park. You said I had the most beautiful vibes you'd ever seen. I still have your tarot card but I don't know where to find you. If you read this, please meet me in front of City Lights Bookstore next Wednesday, Thursday, Friday or Saturday. I'll be waiting. Wheat Germ."

It is known that the paper provided employment for many Aquarians, who were sent into the streets to sell copies to fellow Aquarians and the many tourists from other lands.

ROLLING STONE

A YOUNG Aquarian newspaper reporter, known by the by-line **Wunderkind** Jann Wenner, was largely responsible for this most popular of Aquarian publications. The **"Stone,"** as it was sometimes called, was both a journal of political thought and a bulletin of the latest advances in agriculture.

In addition, Wunderkind Wenner portrayed the leading troubadors of the time on the cover of his magazine, with many households collecting these ornate covers. Evidently, appearing on the cover of the *Rolling Stone* was a symbol of great prestige in Aquarian culture.

A cache of tattered *Rolling Stone*s was found about a mile from the dig site in what was a transmission station for archaic "frequency modulation" radio waves. After painstakingly restoring the brittle pages, our researchers have plotted the editorial progress of the *Rolling Stone* and revealed how it reflected the quickly changing Aquarian world.

In the final issues, the magazine—actually a "tabloid," from the publication genus "scandal sheet"—appears to have shifted its focus from politics and agriculture to profiles of Aquarian and Amerikan celebrities. The explanation for this shift is not to be found within its pages. Also, there are intimations that the base of operations for *Rolling Stone* would be moved from San Francisco to the East Coast of North Amerika.

Researchers have noted the striking similarity between the later *Rolling Stone* and the early *People* magazine of the middle Amerikan culture of the 1980s—the civilization of the "Mall" people—and have hypothesized that *Rolling Stone* may actually have become *People*.

CHAPTER 6

TRANSPORTATION, TRADE AND COMMERCE

BACKPACK

NYLON, PLASTIC, LEATHER, ALUMINUM

DIMENSIONS: (unpacked) 2′ × 4′

INSCRIPTION: "See America (*sic*) First"

THE AQUARIANS were a people greatly interested in travel. Many of the early settlers of Berkeley were from other parts of North Amerika. The fabled nearby city of **Hateashbury** was said be populated solely by inhabitants of other regions.

Most Aquarians would take a long journey by foot or by two-wheeled vehicle—not unlike the "grand tour" of an earlier time—by the age of sixteen, although many were known to have taken this trip even earlier. Due to the lack of surveyors, these young travelers set out to "find Amerika" and returned home to report their findings. In this way they made their rite of passage.

The Aquarian liked to travel light, to allow the greatest possible freedom and mobility. He would rarely carry more than a backpack or duffel bag and usually brought only one set of clothes, relying on the goodwill of those he met for food and lodging. There was rarely a fixed itinerary and the destination could be changed for no apparent reason, so that a traveler on his way to Canada might end up in the tiny country of Vietnam.

Many traveled from the West Coast to the enclave in a great metropolis in the East called the Green Village. Others headed south to Mexico to learn the hemp trade. They brought back planting knowledge and a highly developed system of agricultural economics. Canada was also a popular destination. This was a particularly strange choice since the uneventful Canadian journeys, which were among the longest the Aquarians took, sometimes lasted five to seven years.

The particularly bold traveled across the great eastern oceans to the Isle of Man, where huge tribal gatherings are known to have taken place. Or to Amsterdamn, where there was a large camping facility and a tremendous variety of ritual drugs could be purchased. Some Aquarians ventured even farther, on to Grease, and to Turkey to study horticulture.

ITEM V-8
MAGIC BUS
METAL, RUBBER, PAINT, MORE PAINT
DIMENSIONS: 10′ × 12′ × 35′
INSCRIPTION: "This vehicle stops at railroad crossings."

SEVERAL EXAMPLES of the transportation vehicles of the Aquarians were found in the vicinity of the dig site. The brightly colored vehicles, known as "buses," had the capacity to carry a number of passengers in Spartan comfort. Some were outfitted with sleeping accommodations for overnight long hauls. A few have been found to include crude stoves and sinks as well.

From references in literature and song it is believed that Aquarians used these public transportation vehicles to travel to various ritual festivals or to take extended trips in order to "find themselves." Usually, tickets were subsidized by the local Aquarian leaders or available for a nominal fee.

The major transport lines were known as the **Psychedelic Bus,** the **Magic Bus** and the **Grey Rabbit.** It is thought that a renowned band of minstrels, the **Merry Pranksters,** used public transportation exclusively in their travels. A smaller fleet of "micro" buses owned by the **VW Bus Lines** operated over shorter distances. The exact routes cannot be reconstructed for the various lines as they operated apparently without firm schedules or, for the most part, known destinations.

THE FOUNDATION of the Aquarian economic system was the **Acapulco Gold** standard. All commerce was based on the price of one kilo of imported AG. As this price fluctuated so did the costs of goods and services. During several man-made and natural disasters in the area of the world known as Mexico, a shortage of AG forced the Aquarians to redefine their system, substituting other precious crops such as Panama Red.

The basic units of currency within the society were the nickel and the dime. As the AG standard varied, the nickel and dime would take on different values. At times the nickel and dime were severely devalued, such as when a large number of "seeds" and "stems" began showing up in the cash crops of the Aquarians. At other times, when the "really good shit" (evidently a standard of quality, origin unknown) was available, a dime bag could go for about twenty of our currency units.

The rest of the Aquarian economic system was based on a redistribution of wealth, with many products being provided free. There was also some barter, although as a rule this was restricted to homemade goods. Unfortunately, thievery, which was known as "shoplifting," was rampant in Aquarian society. This social malady was due to fluctuations in the AG standard, which made the entire economic system highly volatile.

ITEM 510

ACAPULCO GOLD STANDARD

CANNABIS, OREGANO, PLASTIC

DIMENSIONS: An ounce

DIORAMA RTE66
OUTLAWS
OF THE AQUARIANS
HARLEY, LEATHER, CHAINS, DIRT
SCALE: Life Size
ARTIST: C. C. Ryder

FROM THE celluloid entertainment *Easy Rider* and the writings of famed sociologist Dr. Hunter Thompson, we have a fairly comprehensive portrait of the "outlaws" of the Aquarians. These rugged individualists were outsiders in the Aquarian culture, although they dressed like Aquarians and enjoyed many of the same recreations.

The most famous of the outlaws were the "easy riders" who roamed the North Amerikan continent in search of high-quality Acapulco Gold (which has led our researchers to believe they were former investment bankers). The perilous journeys they undertook are celebrated in a celluloid entertainment named in their honor. Riding two-wheeled vehicles known as "hoppers," they cruised into the forbidden two-lane blacktop world of the Amerikans.

The two celluloid adventurers of *Easy Rider* met a grisly end when attacked by Amerikan irregulars known as "red-necks",—so named for the colorful bandannas they wore—somewhere in the southern part of Amerika.

Outlaws traveling in large bands and wearing elaborately decorated uniforms also made forays into Amerika. As they approached a town, their Harley-Davidson two-wheeled vehicles emitted a deafening roar, which frightened the villagers away long enough for the gang to sack the town and escape before Amerikan security forces could arrive.

Among the early bandit gangs were "The Wild Ones," with the infamous **Brando** as leader. Later, a confederation of outlaws was formed and came to be known as the **Hell's Angels,** with chapters all across both Aquarian and Amerikan lands. During times of great turmoil within Aquarian culture, this confederation was sometimes called upon to provide security for Aquarians when their own armed forces were unable to do so.

ITEM 438
FOOD COOPERATIVE
METAL, GREEN PAINT, FOOD RESIDUE, METHANE
DIMENSIONS: 4′ × 5′ × 8′
INSCRIPTION: "Trash-Mor Container Service"

TO ENSURE that all segments of the population were properly fed, food cooperatives were set up in bright-green bins that were stationed at the rear of the general-food stores. These bins were open to the public day and night and allowed easy access for the less affluent in search of sustenance.

The basic foodstuffs available from a food cooperative were: day-old bread, dented cans, wilted vegetables and unfrozen frozen foods. With these basic staples the average Aquarian was well nourished in an inexpensive and cooperative way.

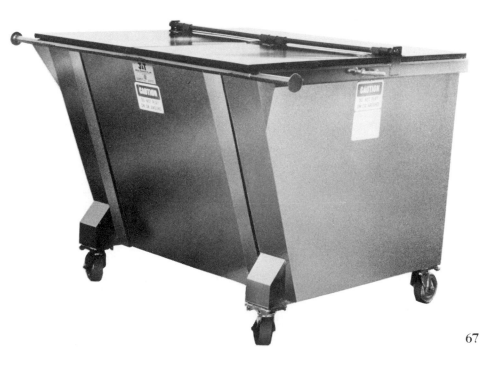

INDIAN PRINT FABRIC
COTTON, NON-COLORFAST DYES
DIMENSIONS: Double; Twin

NOT TO be confused with the aboriginal settlers of the Aquarian homeland, these Indians were from another continent halfway around the world. The establishment of trade with the Indians came about not through exploration or the desire to find new products but through contact with one Maharaji, a mystic, and Ravi Shankar, a musician. The strange teachings of the former and the odd "sitter" music of the latter apparently captured the imagination of the Aquarians.

Indian print fabric of all possible description was rapidly imported from India, and was also copied and produced on a large scale in North Amerika.

This was just the beginning of the Aquarian rage for things Eastern. Entire cults sprang up around the myriad new mystics who seemed to have been imported along with the cloth. These many sects were economically self-sufficient. Indeed, the leaders often became very wealthy through the goodness of their teachings.

CHAPTER 7

RELIGION, CUSTOMS, FESTIVALS AND FOLKLORE

ITEM 418

THE PROPHET

PAPER, INK, CLOTH

DIMENSIONS: $5^{1}/_{2}'' \times 8^{1}/_{4}'' \times 1''$

INSCRIPTION: $7.95

EVERY HOUSEHOLD was required to have a copy of the Aquarian "holy book," which records the teachings of one Kahlil Gibran, the prophet of the Aquarians.

Not much is known about Gibran and there is some speculation that he was not even an Aquarian himself. But the book and its teachings were used by Aquarians to answer the riddles of life and to plan for the future. Gibran diaries, with each day's page headed by a quotation from the great prophet, were found in many of the dwellings of the Aquarians. Gibran's teachings are presented in the form of paradoxical statements which, when unraveled, gave the Aquarian a psychic blueprint for living his life.

Linguists theorize that the divided right-brain/left-brain thinking of the Aquarians explains why the "holy book" had to be paradoxical to be of use. Analysts are currently working to decipher the meaning of Gibran's writings. They hope this information and the understanding that comes from it will be profitable to our own culture.

ITEM MJ303
THE SACRED SYMBOL
SILVER, INLAID TURQUOISE
DIMENSIONS: 1″ × 1¹/₂″

IMPRINTED ON many of the Berkeley artifacts is the sacred symbol of the Aquarians, the hemp leaf. All good was thought to stem from the hemp plant, and indeed economics, recreation and spirituality were all directly affected by it. The leaf was so important to the Aquarians that it was anthropomorphized in tale and song as Mary Jane, in much the same way as the British had centuries before personified John Barleycorn.

Buttons, pottery, patches on clothing and even one of the Aquarian confederation flags were found bearing the three-pronged leaf. Apparently, displaying the leaf symbol in virtually any context was considered **NORML.**

REDS, VITAMIN C, COCAINE

SECONAL, ASCORBIC ACID, COCA LEAF DERIVATIVE

DIMENSIONS: $1/8'' \times 1/2''$; $1/4''$ diameter; "a line"

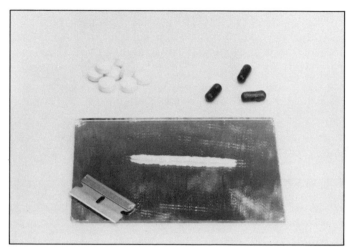

ARCHAEOLOGISTS WERE startled to discover a scattering of materials at Berkeley that gives credence to the legend of a 1960s cult known as the **Dead Heads.** The cult is reputed to have had followers for centuries, but little of its real significance has ever been understood by outsiders. It is known that cult members made use of ceremonial garb, holy songs and ritual drugs, all of which allowed them to realize a concept known as "truckin'."

The dig team was at first terrified by the Dead Head materials, replete with grotesque images of the human skeleton. Superstitiously, they feared a curse of the sort that had fallen upon many of the pioneers of their discipline in Egypt.

Yet no one "freaked." After studying the materials, the scientists concluded that all was benign and that the legend of the Dead Heads being "Friends of the Devil" was most likely fabrication. The cult's sacred literature does reveal, however, that members worshiped an early prophet—one "Pigpen"—although knowledge of his ritual function has been lost.

The high priests of the Cult of the Dead Heads,

led by the bearded Garcia and an "old lady" named Mountain Girl, were a group of traveling minstrels who attracted large crowds whenever they played. (Fragmentary song lyrics disclose that they lived on a diet of "reds, vitamin C and cocaine.")

There are unsubstantiated reports that followers would travel thousands of miles and wait for days outside huge arenas to attend a ritual performance by their leaders. Like the early Christians, many members of the cult are known to have written epistles ("Dead Letters"), although these were never collected in any complete form. The epistles were often elaborately illustrated.

Using the most sophisticated computer analysis, scientists have been able to determine the basic musical forms used by the cult. Simple and repetitious, most are written in 4/4 time with 8-bar breaks and a I-IV-V progression. The repetition was essential to inducing a state of mind known as "mellow," during which followers are said to have had blissful transcendental experiences.

CEREMONIAL LIBATION VESSEL

GLASS, FERMENTED GRAPE JUICE, SUGAR, FORMALDEHYDE

DIMENSIONS: 5″ × 12″

INSCRIPTION: "Serve Very Cold"

THE PRINCIPAL libation vessel of the Aquarians was molded of colorful green glass and imprinted with the words "Boone's Farm" or "Ripple." Evidently, Boone's Farm—probably located north of Berkeley in the wine region just south of the hemp region—was the vineyard where the traditional drink of the Aquarians was made. "Ripple" is thought to have been their primary toast.

The large number of libation vessels strewn about the dig site indicates that each man, woman and child was presented with one at birth to be used on various ceremonial occasions, including the gatherings of the tribes.

Researchers were startled by the analysis of the residue in the vessels. The "nectar" of the Aquarians was apparently a repugnant, sickly sweet and diluted cousin of table wine. Owing to the drink's meager alcohol content, it is highly unlikely that the Aquarians consumed it to become inebriated. They would have had to imbibe enormous amounts from the Boone's Farm vessels to do so.

72

ASTROLOGICAL CHART

PAPER, INK

DIMENSIONS: COSMIC

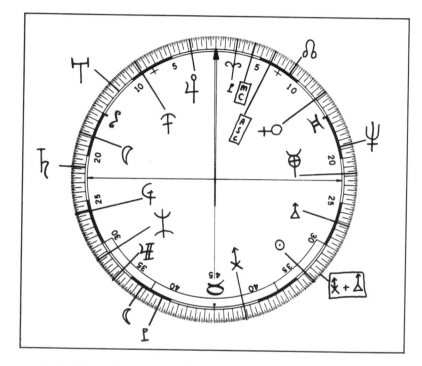

THE AQUARIANS had a highly developed understanding of astrology and applied it to virtually every facet of life. Indeed, the very beginnings of Aquarian culture, as noted in a fragment from one of their tribal songs (which refers to the moon being in the seventh house and Jupiter aligning with Mars), were foretold in the stars.

Aquarians planted their cash crop, hemp, according to the position of the stars. Relationships among Aquarians were largely dictated by the sign under which they were born. Major decisions were based upon which star was rising, and troubadors would often consult astrologers before performing. The Aquarian belief in the importance of astrology was influential in the naming of children. As a result, boys and girls known as "Starshine," "Southern Cross," "Asteroid Field" and "Big Dipper" were not uncommon.

Each Aquarian was aware of his sign; whether he or she was on the cusp; his moon and sun signs; and the longtitude, latitude and exact time of his birth. This basic information was conveyed to other Aquarians in a codified language (for example, "Hey, like I'm a Virgo, man, on the cusp") that would allow other Aquarians to understand and excuse any bizarre behavior. This reduced conflict among the peace-loving Aquarians. Indeed, for them love "steered the stars."

73

"OFF THE PIGS" AMULET
METAL, PLASTIC, INK
DIMENSIONS: Diameter 1″

THIS BUTTON was intended to ward off attacks of the pigs, against whom the Aquarians expressed great bitterness and enmity. Other cultures used similar charms, hoping to drive away disease or evil spirits. Note the resemblance between the button and the snout of a swine.

An attack of the pigs could occur at any time and was known as a "bust." Such an attack might be planned or spontaneous on the part of the pigs, expected or a total surprise. An Aquarian might be "busted" while on a pilgrimage to Washington, during a great battle such as that of Chicago, or really anywhere, anytime in Amerika for just "hanging out" and "doing his own thing." One of the worst sort of pig attacks was the pre-dawn raid on an Aquarian's "pad" and was considered a "real bummer."

Apparently, the pigs had as great a taste for ritual drugs as for truffles, and often would consume the Aquarians' supply. Attacks on rural outposts where hemp was grown, on the supply lines to urban centers such as Berkeley and on ritual-drug distributors at all levels were particularly common.

DIORAMA DC1

WASHINGTON MONUMENT

STONE BLOCKS
SCALE: 1:100
ERECTED 1888

DURING THE 1960s, Aquarians made several mass pilgrimages to the site of the Washington Monument on the East Coast of the continent. The trip must have been one of great hardship, for the Aquarians had to cross many hostile lands only to risk being arrested by Amerikans once they reached the site of the monument.

This, however, did not deter them, for come they did in a massive display of homage to the "father of their country." The pilgrimages were great festivals for the Aquarians, uniting tribes from all over the continent. During one pilgrimage, the Aquarians, perhaps feeling the power of their numbers, attacked the headquarters of the Amerikan forces at the Pentagon Building. They were easily rebuffed. During another pilgrimage they were set upon by Amerikan police, and hundreds of them were locked up in a giant football stadium for many hours.

Pilgrimages to the monument apparently were not annual. They probably occurred when the Aquarians felt the need to renew their spirit by visiting their ancestral homeland—seat of the democracy that they so tried to reform. The pilgrimages took place infrequently toward the end of the Aquarian Age.

FBI MOST WANTED POSTER

PAPER, INK

DIMENSIONS: 8½″ × 11″

INSCRIPTION:
"Armed and extremely dangerous"

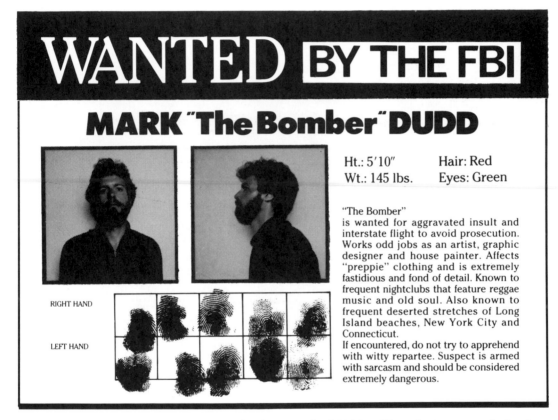

WANTED BY THE FBI

MARK "The Bomber" DUDD

Ht.: 5'10" Hair: Red
Wt.: 145 lbs. Eyes: Green

"The Bomber"
is wanted for aggravated insult and interstate flight to avoid prosecution. Works odd jobs as an artist, graphic designer and house painter. Affects "preppie" clothing and is extremely fastidious and fond of detail. Known to frequent nightclubs that feature reggae music and old soul. Also known to frequent deserted stretches of Long Island beaches, New York City and Connecticut.
If encountered, do not try to apprehend with witty repartee. Suspect is armed with sarcasm and should be considered extremely dangerous.

RIGHT HAND

LEFT HAND

THE AQUARIANS were democratic in spirit for the most part, but apparently could not resist the temptation of singling out particular individuals for special attention.

The **Famous Brave Individuals,** or the **FBI,** were the heroes of Aquarian culture and were afforded unique treatment. When an **FBI Most Wanted** came to town the Aquarian villagers would house and clothe him and keep others from disturbing his privacy. They would give a Most Wanted money and shelter for as long as he needed them and arrange transportation to the Most Wanted's next resting spot.

The FBI Most Wanteds were generally freedom fighters in the various Aquarian **Wars of Oppression,** revered and feared among their own people. Many of them were women. The Most Wanteds were simply the best at what they did, whether it was demolishing buildings, banking or "offing pigs"—an unusual skill since most Aquarians were vegetarians.

Any list, whether best-dressed or Most Wanted, is bound to change with fashion. This was why the Aquarians had picture cards and posters made up for easy reference to help identify a Most Wanted when he or she arrived in town.

COMIX

OF THE many famous anthropomorphic felines of literary and cultural history, there are a select few who reign over the kitty-box pantheon. There was **Puss 'n Boots,** who went to London to visit the Queen. There was **Kliban the Cat,** who looked like a meatloaf. And of course there's the one who survives today, perhaps the greatest grouch of all time, **Garfield.**

But none, perhaps, can compare for licentiousness, tomfoolery and all-round good times with the Aquarians' **Fritz the Cat.** "Comix"—colorfully illustrated books written in the language of Aquarian children—and animated celluloid entertainments sing the praises of this naughty, high-spirited mouser. The Aquarians gave Fritz those qualities that they would have most liked to embody, and never ceased to delight in his escapades.

Other "Comix" entertainers, the Fabulous Furry Freak Brothers, were to the Aquarians what the Marx Brothers and the Three Stooges were to their parents. Delightful, loony characters, the Brothers were constantly getting into difficulties with the local police and women for violating ritual-drug laws and the women. For a time, the FFF Brothers' publication went "underground" because of all the trouble they caused.

Researchers at the Institute Ciné have become extremely fond of the Fritz character and delight in running his celluloids over and over. "Comix" featuring the FFF Brothers are frequently found in the lavatories at the University of Roman à Clef, attesting to their enduring popularity as well.

SIDDHARTHA

PAPER, INK

DIMENSIONS: 5¼" × 8"

INSCRIPTION (handwritten): *"It's even better than Narcissus and Goldmund, man."*

SIDDHARTHA WAS perhaps the archetypal Aquarian wanderer. His journey was thought to be so significant that it was chronicled by one of the great sages of the Aquarians, Hermann Hesse. Many printings of Herr Hesse's account were published for the edification of the Aquarian masses. Here is what can be reconstructed of Siddhartha's tale from recovered fragments:

Like many other young Aquarians, Sid left his wealthy family to pursue a contemplative life in the wilderness. He was seduced by the life of the flesh, however, and fathered an illegitimate child. During a ritual-drug experience, he stumbled to the banks of a river, sickened by lust and greed and wanting to die.

Then a voice came to him. It was Govinda, his "faithful, anxious" friend, "talking him down" and saving his life. Govinda had followed a more conventional path in life than Sid. Did Govinda persuade Sid to adopt a more traditional life-style? Was Sid happy in the end? Unfortunately, these are questions to which we shall never have the answers, since the final pages are missing.

UPON THE founding of Woodstock Nation, the leaders of the fledgling union decided they needed a rallying song to unite the Aquarian tribes. They approached the troubador Jimmy Hendrix, asking him to write a national anthem and to perform it at the "constitutional convention" meeting for three days at Woodstock, New York.

A furious debate, however, is thought to have raged at the convention over the final choice of the national anthem. Besides Hendrix's composition, suggested anthems included "Hey Mr. Tambourine Man," "Born to Be Wild" and "Volunteers."

Despite protests by many, Hendrix's new national anthem—a free-form piece of music without lyrics—was performed on the last day of the convention. Unfortunately, due to a massive rain storm, very few delegates were still in Woodstock to hear the performance.

ITEMS 3405–3408
SYMBOL OF
CONFEDERATION
RING, BUTTONS, ARM PATCH
PLASTIC, METAL, CLOTH, INK, DYE
DIMENSIONS: Various

POLITICALLY, THE Aquarians seem to have been a loose confederation of tribes, although references to a "Woodstock Nation" have been discovered in literature and song originating after 1969. A spectacular three-day festival staged that year in eastern North Amerika served to unite the tribes on a platform of "peace, love and music."

The symbol of confederation was ubiquitous throughout Aquarian culture. Since it had no standard color or size, it could accommodate various tribal or individual perferences, and its uses were innumerable.

It was emblazoned on flags and banners, for example, which served to lead the Aquarian armed forces into battle, or to identify various tribal groups at festivals. It decorated "T-shirts," buttons, posters, rings, headbands, belts and countless other objects. Reproduced in every medium and material known to the Aquarians, it also identified tribal members traveling in foreign and sometimes hostile territories.

It was even superimposed on what was apparently the flag of another nation, whose primary colors were red, white and blue. Historians speculate that the country may have been Amerika, against which the Aquarians fought many of their greatest battles.

ITEM 4481

PORT-O-SAN
WOOD, STEEL, PLASTIC
DIMENSIONS: 4′ × 4′ × 7′9″

INSCRIPTION: "Mobile Comfort Station"

EXTENSIVELY RESTORED

FOUND IN great numbers near the site of the Wood-stock Constitutional Convention, these strange moveable objects have also been located as far west as the famous Aquarian blacktop racing strip for gasoline-powered vehicles with funny shapes, known as Altamont Speedway.

This particular example was found at the edge of a large grassy field not far from several concrete pillars embedded in the ground. The pillars are thought to have been part of a giant stage where the proceedings of the Convention took place. But how the Aquarians, without benefit of modern technology, could have dragged these concrete pillars many miles over difficult terrain is still a mystery.

Each Port-O-San contained a plastic or metal bowl and a holding tank, often bearing the residue of a fragrant chemical compound no longer in use. It is theorized that Port-O-Sans were portable offertoria. Further testing of the chemical remains in the bowls and tanks should confirm the theory.

81

CHAPTER 8

LEISURE AND SPORT

ITEM 791

TOLKIEN ON VACATION

SCALE: 1:1

PHOTOGRAPHER: F. Baggins

THE AQUARIANS, like other twentieth-century cultures, were taken with the archaic notion of the "vacation." Based on the rather complete travel guide found at the dig, researchers concluded that **Middle Earth** must have been the Aquarians' first choice as a vacation land.

In this volume, the guide Frodo leads the reader through the mystical, wonderful land that Middle Earth must have been. The book also provides a brief summary of all the living inhabitants of Middle Earth, which must have made meeting new friends in the vacation land easy.

Middle Earth was populated by strange beings known as Hobbits. It is interesting to note that the Mt. Doom described in the Middle Earth travel guide is remarkably similar to the Bald Mountain depicted in the popular celluloid entertainment of the Aquarians, *Fantasia.*

The favorite souvenirs of a journey to Middle Earth were rings. Aquarians might bring back anywhere from one to nine of the trinkets. It is thought that Middle Earth became the favored vacation spot for Aquarians after they were barred from their previous first choice, **Disneyland,** because of their dress. Researchers have never been able to locate Middle Earth, although Disneyland is thought to have been situated somewhere in what was known as **SoCal.**

THE REMARKABLE CANINES OF THE AQUARIANS

SCALE: Life Size

CAUTION: Step Carefully Around the Diorama—True to Life in Every Detail

AS THE cat was to ancient Egyptian Earth culture, the dog was to the Aquarians. The canine was frequently treated as a member of the family unit, likely to be fed before any other member. Indeed, the canine was accorded more respect in many cases than the Aquarians' "old ladies."

These remarkable beasts were each given a ceremonial scarf, which was worn about the animal's neck as a sign of his lofty position. The most revered of all canines was the "mutt," which was known to be able to chase saucer objects for great distances, leaping up with a full extension of the body to wrest the saucer from the air.

Some Aquarian family units were known to keep several dogs in the household, but the animals were never truly domesticated so as to preserve their sacred position as "free spirits." They were allowed access to all portions of the house to roam and defecate in at will. It was only natural.

GAME OF TAROT

PAPER, INK

DIMENSIONS: 3″ × 4¹/₂″

INSCRIPTION: "Property of Madame Wu"

THE MAGICIAN.

THESE BEAUTIFULLY designed playing cards were discovered within a foundation that has since been identified as the residence of Madame Wu, apparently an adviser to the Aquarians who was also quite a gambler. Rather than hearts, clubs, diamonds and spades, the suits represented by the surviving examples were "cups," "wands," "swords" and "pentacles." Otherwise, tarot is thought to have been similar to other twentieth-century card games.

It is believed that the game required four players and that each one was dealt twelve of the seventy-eight available cards, with the extra thirty being placed facedown in the center of the table. The object was to match pairs and eliminate them from one's hand. Players unable to make a match would be told to "Go Fish" in the center pile. As in "Old Maid," the ultimate goal was to avoid ending up with a certain card. In tarot, this was the "Death" card.

"STRIKE" SYMBOL

THIS STENCILED symbol is thought to have indicated the location of an upcoming boxing match, boxing being a sport the Aquarians used to channel their aggressive tendencies. The history of the champions of Aquarian boxing is lost to us. It is assumed, however, that like most activities the Aquarians engaged in, boxing was governed by a loose set of rules.

Perhaps local champions of the tribe would arrange for a match on short notice and the "strike" symbol ("strike" evidently being the Aquarian word for boxing) would be stenciled on the building in which the match was to take place. University buildings were thought to be the usual arena for the matches.

Since the Aquarians were basically a peace-loving people, boxing, or "striking," must have been a far less savage sport than the one which we know today. Indeed, scholars gather that during some strikes the participants repaired to the office of the university dean, smoking cigars and drinking fine brandy between rounds.

85

AQUABED
VINYL, HYDROGEN DIOXIDE, BRASS
DIMENSIONS OF ACTUAL BED: 8' × 8'
INSCRIPTION: "Do not puncture"

ONE OF the great technological advances of the ages took place in Aquarian times. After centuries of sleeping on hard floors, torn mattresses or even on the concrete sidewalks, the Aquarians developed a plastic bed filled with an aqueous solution.

This breakthrough totally changed the way of life of the Aquarians. Instead of getting up each day ill-rested, they enjoyed the newfound sensation of a soft, rolling ocean under their bodies. They began spending more and more time in bed. Business was conducted from the bed, as was ritual-drug taking.

Whether the mother of invention was necessity in this case is hard to assess. It is interesting to note, however, that this dramatic change in the prone behavior of the Aquarians coincided almost exactly with the "summer of love."

SELECTIVE SERVICE CARD

PAPER, INK, LIGHTER FLUID
DIMENSIONS: Wallet Size
INSCRIPTION: "Required by Law to Have in Your Possession"

To AID the many thousands of their young men who wished to explore the world, the Aquarians instituted a lottery system that would send selected individuals on all-expenses-paid trips. Each young man was assigned a **Selective Service Number** and was required to keep his **Selective Service Card** on his person at all times, for he never knew when he might be "called up." To be "called up" was apparently such a high honor that the Aquarians became incensed when a young man refused the opportunity, and would fine and imprison him.

Two locations were favored above all others by the **Selective Service Commission**—Vietnam and Germany. Unfortunately, traveling fellowships to Vietnam were more widely available than to

Germany, yet Germany was a much more popular destination among the Aquarian young men. They campaigned vigorously for Canada and Sweden to be added to the list of possible destinations, but to no avail.

Each year a holiday was set aside on which Selective Service lottery numbers would be chosen for the following year. Young Aquarians would gather suspensefully about The Tube to witness the lottery selections. Those who were granted their desired destination would celebrate wildly with friends and family. Others not so fortunate might become so upset that they would actually burn their Selective Service Cards.

EPILOGUE
The Role of the Aquarians in the Rise of the Quiche Eaters

Wheat flour,
¹/₄ lb. sliced bacon,
2 cups cream,
3 whole eggs,
¹/₄ teaspoon salt,
1 teaspoon chopped chives,
¹/₂ cup diced Swiss cheese

It is uncertain what became of Aquarian culture in the decades and centuries following the 1960s, since to date very few artifacts from that later period have been discovered, except encoded magnetic diskettes known as "software." Perhaps the Aquarians' descendants were so involved in the production of software that they left very little hard evidence of their culture behind. We do not know whether the Aquarians continued to thrive or whether their civilization declined quickly, like so many others, eventually to be forgotten completely. We do have evidence, however, that in at least one realm of culture—diet—the Aquarians of the 1960s profoundly influenced their immediate successors.

In their search for alternatives to the unhealthy foods available from the neighboring Amerikans, the Aquarians ransacked the cuisines of their known world. From the land of the Francs came the **quiche,** a pie based on eggs and dairy products. The consumption of quiche was consistent with the Aquarians' prevailing vegetarianism, although apparently bits of cooked pig were sometimes added in the form of "bacon." Copious use of onions and other strong flavorings in the quiches necessitated frequent cleaning of the teeth with Arm & Hammer Baking Soda.

Another food that the Aquarians ate frequently was **sprouts.** Outstanding work by agricultural specialists has traced the origin of sprouts not merely to Francland's neighbor, Belle-Gym, but to its very capital, Brussels. From Nippon and Chiner came **tofu,** a versatile but criminally bland high-protein bean curd paste.

All of these items were found on the menu of an eating establishment (also uncovered during recent construction activity near Berkeley) whose remains date from no earlier than 1977. The restaurant was of the "fern barn" type, so called because of the many fern fossils found within it. The featured food of the restaurant was indicated by its name—Quicheteria—and by the menu, which offered more than twenty varieties of the Franc-ish pie.

This evidence has led historians to dub the immediate descendants of the Aquarians the Quiche Eaters. We have too little information at this time to determine whether the Quiche Eaters represented a truly distinct culture, or were merely a decadent footnote to the Aquarian Age. It is hoped that someday we will understand the Quiche Eaters as well as we now do the Aquarians.

FOR THE MUSEUM

Thomas Heaving Diggerhalter
Curator of North Amerikan Antiquities, Metroplex Museum of Art.

Attended Hardyard University, Institute of Old Things at Oxnard University and the Sorebone. Formerly married to socialite Amanda Bailout. Two children: Clay and Grave. Constant companion: Lotte Peel, conceptual computer artist. Dig supervisor at Indiana Indian Mound and the Mars Canal excavation. Fear of "little green men" forced Diggerhalter to give up dig-site supervision in favor of cocktail circuit supervision.

Ann O. Graham
Cryptologist, Ecrest University.

PP.D.(Doctor of Puns and Puzzlements) from Palindrome U. Three-time winner of the Interplanetary Crossword Puzzle Contest, solving her final puzzle in a record 2.68 seconds. Lives with her four cats: Riddle, Conundrum, Perplexity and Mr. Stumped. Along with her research assistant, Rosetta Stone, she has deciphered the colorful scrawling from New York Subway Car 033 on display at the Metroplex last spring.

François Explicateur
Literary critic and third assistant deputy director of L'École Gobbledegook at the Sorebone.

Treatise on wildflower and grass imagery in the novels of Thomas Hardy is now a classic. Cataloged punctuation mistakes in the works of Roland Barthes. Member of the Club Literati. Undergraduate degree from L'Institut Sacré Bleu. M.I.D. (Master of Insignificant Detail) and RLA.D. (Doctor of Ridiculous Literary Assumptions) from Picayune University, New Orleans.

H. Word Smith
Etymologist, University of Roman à Clef.

Received first-class honors at Hogsford University for his work in Munchkin etymology more than a hundred years ago. Last year received the *Curmudgeonly but Kindly Scholar Award* from former students. Amuses at faculty parties by reciting Dr. Johnson's dictionary backward. Rumored to have a list of 1,400 words for female genitalia.

Pan Dantic
Chairman of USHTUL (Universal Symposium of Hard-to-Understand Literature), University of Roman à Clef.

Undergraduate and graduate degrees from the University of Roman à Clef, where he specialized in reading *Finnegans Wake*. Founded USHTUL in an effort to bring the complexities of ancient and modern literature to the masses. Novelist in his own right: *Peter Paragon*, a novel in which every word begins with the letter *P*; *Along the Riverrun*, a parody of James Joyce's work in which every river, lake and pond on Earth is mentioned at least twice; *Mirror, Mirror* which can be read only when held up to a mirror.

O.L.D. Fossil
Dig supervisor, Metroplex Museum of Art.

Undergraduate career at the University of Pentupmania interrupted after funds were denied him for his projected *Hole to China* dig. Explored Panama, Suez and Guadal Canals as a member of the university's "For a Change" program.

Dyllar Tante
Graduate student, University of Pentupmania.

Obtained position under dig-team supervisor through long friendship of father, Bon Vivant Tante, with Thomas Heaving Diggerhalter. Uniquely endowed for her restoration work by successfully completing course 437, "Removing Crusty Dirt from Small Things." After suffering a "twisted ankle" on the first day of the dig, she was forced to spend many uncomfortable weeks on her back.

Orchid Fonde
Chief sifter, Metroplex Museum of Art.

Unpretentious daughter of the mega-wealthy *Fonde Du* family (she has dropped the aristocratic suffix), Orchid is a self-taught sifter, having spent a childhood combing the finest beaches. Along with her dig-site work, she has single-handedly embarked on an ambitious plan to drain the fouled canals of Venice.

S. Muggler
Chief of dig-site security.

His promising career as an archaeologist was curtailed when in a student prank he and fellow classmates tried to pass off a "plaid jumper" as the original clothing of the Kiltdown man. Remorseful for this breach of ethics, he has devoted his life to the prevention of black-market sales of antiquities. He will frequently transport precious objects in his own luggage and has been invaluable in preventing rival museums from acquiring items bound for the Metroplex Museum.

Illinois Smythe
Film archivist, Institut Ciné.

Adventurer and lover of romance, Illinois Smythe seems out of place behind his horn-rimmed glasses in the basement of the Institut Ciné. One of the few remaining practitioners of the art of celluloid entertainment analysis, he is also an on-site member of the dig team. He is generally credited with the quick recovery of the injured Dyllar Tante.

PHOTOGRAPHY CREDITS AND PERMISSIONS

ACKNOWLEDGMENTS

There are many people without whom this book would not have been possible. First, our editor, Gerry Howard, whose knowledge of the 1960s, cogent suggestions, sense of humor and enthusiasm for this project were tremendously appreciated. We are also grateful for the interest and support of Alan Kellock, Brenda Marsh, Dan Farley, Pam Walker and many others at Viking Penguin too numerous to list here.

We thank our designer, Ken Diamond of Art Patrol, Lloyd Miller of Art Patrol, and our photographer, Leighton Miller, for their excellent work, creativity and good humor.

A large debt of gratitude is owed to the many relatives, friends, and friends of friends who gave so generously of their time, energy, attics and closets in locating and lending props, in serving as models, in making helpful suggestions, and in providing warm support. They include: Phebe Anderson, Bob Bender, Matt Callaway, Ty Danco, Michele Farinet, Bob Gilbert, Lucy Handley, Cindy Hawkins, Elizabeth Hughes, Kate Kelly, Maureen Kelly, K. C. Kelly, Victoria Klose, Evan Lambert, Carol Livingston, Maggie Mae, Jane Meara, Hal Morgan, Larry Norton, Wayne Pannabecker, Walker Richardson, Meg Ruley, Elizabeth Saslow, Bert Snyder, Anne Stone, Greg Stone, Sue Stone, Liz Strach, Kerry Tucker, David Varney, Pat Varney, David Wachs, and Laura Worsham.

We would also like to thank the many businesses, agencies and individuals who kindly provided us with props and photographs. Their contributions are gratefully enumerated on the preceding page.

The manuscript for this book was composed on a TRS-80 Model III Microcomputer.

PENGUIN BOOKS

TREASURES OF THE AQUARIANS

Richard Davis was born in 1953, raised near Chicago and educated at the College of Du Page and the University of Illinois. Jeff Stone was born in 1955 in Providence, Rhode Island, grew up in Maine and graduated from Brown University. After several years in book publishing, they founded East Chelsea Press, a book-production company in New York City. They are co-authors of *Growing Up Catholic* and *What Color Is Your Toothbrush?*, and are also currently developing an original television series.